Fiddlers Fling

Endorsements for Fiddlers Fling

I loved it. It was a great read, and not easy to put down. I loved the storyline, and it was interesting, easy to get caught up in. Demonstrates the love between a father and daughter, no matter what has happened, as well as how life tends to "happen," even when we're not right there with our family, friends, etc. Also depicts the beauty of faith throughout life and in all circumstances, and the promise that God forgives, no matter how human we are.

Being the daughter of an Old Time Fiddler in the NYS Hall of Fame, I so enjoyed the role that music plays in this story. Growing up in a fiddling family, the similarities to our jam sessions and fiddle contests brought back fond memories for me, as well as the mention of familiar tunes such as "Orange Blossom Special" and "Ashokan Farewell." Congratulations on another wonderful book, Linda!
—**Maria Boyea Bourgeois**, a Fiddler's Daughter

Literary and lovely, the twists and turns of Rondeau's *Fiddlers Fling* will keep you turning pages to the satisfying end.
—**Carol McClain**, author

Fiddlers Fling tells the story of an embattled rivalry between the families of engaged couple Jolene Murdock, a small-town girl, and Robert Ashworth, a wealthy politician. Twists and turns abound throughout the book as mysteries tease the reader. Linda Rondeau writes great characterizations and plot, holding my interest throughout the book.
—**Jo Huddleston**, author

Get ready for a complicated romance. It starts with a hard-headed father and his stubborn daughter, Jolene. Add in a gross lack of communication between Jolene and her sweetheart, and you have a situation ripe for a power-hungry family to step in and really complicate matters. This is *Fiddlers Fling*, the story of a young woman torn between the lap of luxury and the comfort of small-town tradition. Rondeau creates characters with conflicting emotions, people you will come to know and care about. You will take sides in the struggles, and you won't want to put this story down until you find out how the complications are resolved.

—**James R. Callan**, award-winning, multi-published author

Fiddlers Fling is a fantastic read, the sort of book you want to snuggle up with. It pulls you in from the get-go as all Jolene's wedding plans are thrown into disarray. Moving back home wasn't on the agenda, but as always God has a plan where we don't. A keeper, it's gone straight back into my to be read pile.

—**Clare Revell**

Linda has done it again. This novel's characters are appealing and attractive, the plot interesting and intriguing. I'm once again impressed with the way Linda's writing captures my attention and holds it, making me unwilling to quit reading for necessary chores and duties.

There is something homey, talented, and brilliant in Linda's stories. They firmly place the reader in the novel setting and won't let them go. You feel as if you're "right there," taking in the situation, feeling the emotions of the characters, and unwilling to close the door on another chapter. And another …

I heartily endorse this book and Rondeau's writing. Once captured by it, you will not be sorry to become an avid fan of her books.

—**Carole Brown**, award-winning, bestselling author

I loved *Fiddlers Fling* by Linda Wood Rondeau. The web of secrets and lies entangled more than one generation of two families, building walls that were hard to tear down. Rondeau created flawed characters who needed to face their fears and memories before reconciliation of any kind could happen. These are characters that pulled me into their story from the first page. I highly recommend this book.

—**Lena Nelson Dooley**, award-winning author

As a faithful member of our worship choir, Linda's love for music is very evident. In *Fiddlers Fling*, Linda has beautifully woven her passion for music and the glorious truth of God's grace and redemption into a touching love story.

Fiddlers Fling

Linda Wood Rondeau

PUBLISHING THE POSITIVE

ELK LAKE PUBLISHING INC
Plymouth, Massachusetts

"Those who sow in tears will reap in joy." Psalm 136:5 NKJV

Cover Design and Interior Design: Derinda Babcock

Editor(s): Kathi Macias, Deb Haggerty

Author Represented by Hartline Literary Agency

PUBLISHED BY: Elk Lake Publishing, Inc., 35 Dogwood Dr., Plymouth, MA 02360, 2018

Library Cataloging Data

Names: Rondeau, Linda Wood (Linda Wood Rondeau

Fiddlers Fling / Linda Wood Rondeau

208 p. 23cm × 15cm (9in × 6 in.)

Description: Jolene Murdock, estranged from her father, leaves home to start a new life. But the past won't leave her alone, drawing her back to the town she fled to care for her father ... and perhaps an old romance.

Identifiers: ISBN-13: 978-1-948888-72-1 (trade) | 978-1-948888-73-8 (POD) | 978-1-948888-74-5 (e-book.)

Key Words: Fiddle, abortion, politics, family, romance, estrangement, forgiveness.

LCCN: 2018959777 Fiction

The thing which counts is the striving of the human soul to achieve spiritually the best that it is capable of and to care unselfishly not only for personal good, but for the good of all those who toil with them upon the earth.

—Eleanor Roosevelt from *The Forum*.

Dedication

To John, Edie, and Jim—Thanks for the adventure!
Love, Mom

Prologue

Jolene Murdock hopped around her room like a two-year-old at Christmas. No small thing to be offered a job at the most prestigious law firm in Albany. The cell slipped from her grasp. "Oh, spinach," she shrieked, emulating Eleanor Roosevelt's substitution for unladylike swear words. Jolene caught her lifeline, the portal to her world, a split-second before it met a watery end in her fish tank.

On the other end, Robert Ashworth clicked impatience. "I sense you have reservations?"

"No. Not at all." *Calm down, girl.* "Tell me more."

"You'll head up our charitable foundation, oversee our donations, arrange fundraisers for recipients, and be an ambassador of good will. Your social-work degree will be an asset."

"I'm not a certified social worker ... yet. I only have my bachelor's degree."

"You can get your master's in Albany. My father's firm will pay for your tuition. Take a few seconds if you need to."

She'd already made her decision. Instead of revealing her giddiness, she took the allowed few seconds to examine the downs, if there were any besides the fact her father would never approve. The strangeness of it all should be considered. Why did Robert's father want to hire her, Jolene Murdock, a simple girl from Brookside? Granted, she'd graduated with honors from Vassar, no small feat. And she was the daughter of the Democratic Chair for Essex County. She'd been a protégé of Robert's mother since the summer following high school graduation—a woman who bolstered Jolene's confidence like the mother Jolene never had. So, why not her? Maybe she really was the perfect choice for the position. But what about Robert? Did he want Jolene to be hired, or had his mother put him up to it? He was three years older than she, and they'd been an item her freshman year, in spite of her father's insistence she not date older boys.

Daddy needn't have worried. Once Robert took off for Harvard, she saw him only a few times, generally at some political function and always with his mother.

The silence grew awkward, and the sounds of drumming fingers carried over Robert's phone into Jolene's ear. "I need an answer. What do I tell my father?"

"Tell him I accept."

"You'll need to pack your bags and take the train to Albany tomorrow. You start Monday."

"That soon?"

"Nothing to gain by waiting. You can pick up your ticket at the station. We've arranged for you to stay in the empty guest house on our estate."

Her doubts resurfaced, and she had to voice them. "Why me, Robert? There must be a slew of candidates far more qualified."

"Mother recommended you to Dad, and she thought hiring someone from Brookside an absolute necessity. She hopes you'll become interested enough in politics to help with my campaign for city council."

"Of course, I will."

"Alicia Davenport is my campaign manager."

Brookside's version of Lucrezia Borgia. "I remember her. She graduated a year ahead of you, as I recall."

"She's a fantastic campaign manager. Majored in political science at Georgetown and interned at the White House. I'm lucky to have someone with her qualifications."

Knowing Alicia, adorned with long black hair and the poster image for Fitness Gym, luck probably had little to do with her hire any more than her long list of credentials served as a basis for Robert's admiration.

"What should I bring with me?"

"Just a few changes. Mother intends to take you shopping as soon as you get here. She's looking forward to teaching you the latest fashions. I sometimes think she wishes I'd been a girl. She considers you as a daughter."

In truth, Mary Ashworth had given Jolene a second birth when life had been at its lowest.

"Great. We'll see you tomorrow." Robert disconnected, and she imagined him checking off this call on a list of tasks, going on to the next. Besides, he probably hadn't expected any other answer than the one she gave. No one refused an Ashworth.

In this case, she'd accepted, not from intimidation but rather opportunity. Who wouldn't be thrilled to head up the Ashworth Foundation?

Now ... how to tell Daddy.

Why couldn't he see the good? The Ashworths had treated her with nothing but kindness. She'd judge them based on her own interactions, not hand-me-down mistrust. Besides, if Daddy had his way, she'd marry Dwight Etting and give her father half a dozen grandchildren. Of course, Daddy would be hurt if she didn't play a duet with him in the upcoming Fiddlers Fling. He'd already cleared off a spot in the trophy case next to their last first-place finish.

Mary Ashworth had been right. "My dear," she'd said, "if you want to do something meaningful with your life, cast off your country ways. No one will take you seriously with a fiddle in your hand."

Daddy must come to terms that his little girl's dreams did not include Brookside.

She'd fix him a pot roast for supper before she broke the news during dessert. Apple pie—his favorite. She glanced out the window at the blackening clouds. A late afternoon thunderstorm meant he'd quit work early. As he always did when he came home, he'd start asking questions before the screen door closed. "What did you do today? Did you find a job yet? If not, you can always work for me. You handle a set of tools better than half the men I have working for me."

The hard thud of the back door jolted her back from her musings and added to her worries.

"Jolene!" His tone scolded as if she'd taken the ATV without permission. Could he have heard about her job offer already?

She blew resolve and took the main staircase to the living room, glaring at the peeling paint, the walls suddenly grotesque with sameness, every room a dull off-white. Daddy stood by his treasured trophy case, a roaring lion protecting his den. His face burned with anger. "Is it true what I hear?"

"What?"

"You and that Ashworth boy?"

"I don't know what you mean."

"Ken Etting said he heard about you and young Ashworth dancing at the ball last night."

"Where did he hear that?"

"From Dwight."

Fiddlers Fling

"Dwight was there?" *And he couldn't even speak to me?*

"He's home on leave. Went to the ball in his father's place since I don't dance anything except a jig, and neither does Ken."

"I didn't see him."

"That's too bad 'cause you should have been dancing with Dwight and not that Ashworth boy.

"That Ashworth boy is named Robert. Why can't you say his name?"

"'Cause he's cut from the same dirty cloth as his father."

The same condemnation she'd heard since high school, which didn't deserve a response.

Chapter One

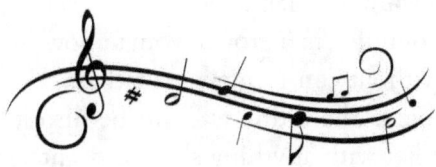

The thought niggled like a stuck piece of broccoli between the teeth. If Dwight saw her last night, she didn't see him because he avoided her. "How long will Dwight be in town?"

"Left again this morning. Going for another tour in Afghanistan. I always liked that boy. Shame you two broke up."

"Dwight Etting wants nothing to do with me. His choice ... not mine."

Big Mike Murdock and Ken Etting blue-printed their children's lives like constructing a house. Dwight probably enlisted more in rebellion than from a broken heart. Any dream of continuing the Murdock-Etting dynasty died on prom night when Dwight ran off in a jealous rage because she'd danced one time with the visiting Robert Ashworth.

Jolene met her father's hard gaze. "Robert Ashworth isn't romantically interested in me."

"I'm not so sure of that. Seems like he manages to talk to you every time he's in town. That boy is sweet on you. A father knows these things."

She'd never won an argument with Daddy. Still, she plowed ahead, right over the boulder in front of them. "It was just a couple of waltzes. Nothing more."

He stared her down. As a little girl, she'd become convinced he could read her mind. Even now, he seemed to know his daughter told him only a half-truth. "Out with it, Jolene."

She sat on the couch. "You'd better sit."

"Nope. Never did take bad news sittin' down. Spit it out. Rip it off like a bandage, I always say."

Fiddlers Fling

"Robert's father offered me a job in Albany. I start Monday."

She expected him to pound his fist on the end table. Instead, he paled and clutched his chest as if she'd stabbed him with a kitchen knife. He raised his head as he cocked it to one side. "Fine time to tell me. Only been three days since you graduated. I planned a party tomorrow after church. Supposed to be a surprise. Only I guess the surprise is on me."

"I got the call five minutes ago. How could I tell you about a job offer that hadn't happened yet?"

"I forbid you to work for them."

She stood her ground. "I'm a grown woman now. You can't forbid me."

"You accepted without consulting your father?"

Her knees wobbled. She didn't want to be disrespectful—not to the man who'd lavished her with anything she ever wanted. "I'm twenty- two. I think for myself now."

He slammed a fist into the wall, cracking the plaster, and stormed from the kitchen and up the stairs. She heard the loud slam of his bedroom door, a clue he'd not budge until she apologized, a tactic he'd used since she was a toddler. His tantrums no longer held power over her.

She wiped angry tears from her eyes as she headed back to her room. She couldn't stay here tonight. Not with tensions so high. Might as well find a hotel and leave for Albany as arranged. She threw a few changes of clothes into her paisley tote that doubled as a purse, and left, slamming the door behind her. A sound like thunder caused her to turn. She gasped at the sight.

The door window had cracked from bottom to top.

(Three Years later)

Jolene closed her biography on Eleanor Roosevelt, a book she valued as much as others treasured their Bibles—always near, highlighted passages, and memorized inspiration. She flexed her fingers, her engagement ring catching her eye, the bling decadent, embarrassingly huge, and ostentatious. Why did Robert think she'd even want something the size of a marble? She hoped he'd catch on to her taste when she ogled the more delicate, heart-shaped ones while window-shopping. However, if this was the ring Robert chose to declare his love, so be it. She'd wear the ring in public and when with him, but nothing in the rule book said she had to wear a huge gem in the privacy of her own quarters.

She took off the diamond and placed the ring next to the simple, white-clothed jewelry box she'd bought at Pottery Barn during one of her rebellious moments. She hid the box in the top drawer of her San Marino Chest, away from Mother Mary's prying eyes, and locked the drawer.

Jolene returned to the living room and stretched out on the Chelsea-Upholstered Chaise and thumbed through the stacks of photos. Alicia had been insistent on the assignment to memorize Albany's aristocracy so Jolene would recognize these important people at Robert's fundraiser tomorrow night. A quick study, she memorized faces and names within an hour.

Yawning, she threw the photos on the cream-colored rug, then ran her hand along the chaise—the red and gold, leafy brocade surface dizzying, the whole of her living area at the mercy of Mother Mary, how she now wanted her future daughter-in-law to address her. Jolene would have preferred Early American as opposed to that of despots. She shuddered at the Louise Moillon still-life displayed behind the chaise. How did anyone consider foodstuffs the ilk of art? The painting, in spite of the artist's perfection, did little to inspire Jolene except to make her hungry.

A craving for apple cider tea sent her into the kitchen, the only room in the house that kept a simple design, the walnut cabinetry unadorned, the island topped with plain white marble. She selected and inserted a caramel-apple-cider pod into her Keurig. While the tea brewed, she checked her messages—three from Robert and two from Mother Mary, probably instructions for Robert's upcoming campaign appearance.

Guilt riddled her conscience as she thought of Eleanor's sophisticated dedication to her husband's ambition. A fiancée should help her intended in his occupation, yet the constant barrage of fundraisers, forced smiles, handshakes, and insincere platitudes had become wearisome. She'd accepted Mr. Ashworth's offer of employment to change the world, not to spend hours getting coiffures, shopping for evening gowns, and modeling for public relations specialists to assure she appeared at her best for the cameras.

She put her iPhone down on the island and sniffed the comforting scent as her selection brewed. Though the calendar said early June, the aroma reminded her of a North-Country winter treat. Sometimes, regret crept on her like black clouds before a thunderstorm. Yet Brookside and Daddy were in her past. No purpose in longing for lost things. She closed her eyes and willed herself back into submission. Her atonement required commitment to her chosen path in spite of the dreariness of public scrutiny.

Her cell vibrated, inching across the counter like a snarky child, displaying a Brookside exchange she didn't recognize. She picked up the phone before it crept to the edge and fell to the floor.

"Jolene."

"Finally."

"Finally."

The voice ... especially its vibrato ... seemed familiar, yet distant, like a dream. "Who is this?"

"Dwight Etting."

Her back stiffened. A ghost from long ago, someone she'd tried hard to forget. "If you've called to apologize for prom night, you're seven years too late."

"I'm not calling about the prom."

Even so, an apology would have made her day regardless of its tardiness. Of course he'd called for some other reason. She paced the kitchen, contemplating whether to continue the call or disconnect. Curiosity kept her on the line in spite of remembered humiliation, as raw now as then. "You ditched me on the most important night of my life."

"I would think a wedding highly more important than a dance." His tone bordered on accusatory yet tempered by a muted cadence. Pity? Why would Dwight Etting think her someone in need of his compassion?

"You know Robert and I are engaged, right?"

"I'm not as smart as you, but I do read the paper. How is our old buddy Ashworth?"

Jolene sensed Dwight's sarcasm. She'd retort right back, make him regret his lack of ambition. "Soon to be New York State Senator Robert Ashworth."

"Don't expect me to vote for him or congratulate you, either." Some things never changed. Tides came and went, and Dwight Etting remained the most annoying man on earth. "Why did you call? I'm assuming it's not to offer campaign support or to congratulate me on my engagement."

"It's about your father."

"I haven't seen him in three years and haven't spoken to him since I called to let him know Robert proposed. He said nothing and hung up on me. Is something wrong?"

An awkward silence before he spoke again. "I don't know where to start, Jolene." His tone resumed a tender undercurrent.

"My father used to say the best way to deliver bad news is to rip it, like tearing off a bandage."

"Big Mike's not managing well."

"That's kind of vague, Dwight. What do you mean by not managing?"

"He's holed himself up in the house. Doesn't open the door and chases anyone away he doesn't want to see. I have a key, and he lets a neighbor lady in. That's it."

She shivered. "How long has this been going on?"

"Been getting worse over the past year. A neighbor brings food over and cleans for him. Otherwise, he'd starve to death or suffocate from the stench. I try to stop in once a day, keep him updated on the business. He refuses to come to our work sites and won't sign any paperwork."

What Dwight didn't say struck the deepest chord. She didn't want to know. Knowing required her to confront the past she'd managed to sanitize through filtered recollection.

"Why are you involved? Last I knew, you were in Afghanistan. Daddy always listened to your father, considered him much more than a partner."

Dwight hesitated. "You didn't know?"

"Know what?"

"My father passed a year ago. Now I'm the Etting in Murdock & Etting. Still only a junior partner, though, and Big Mike still treats me like a kid."

Daddy should have told her—though she could have kept better track of Brookside news. She'd let the Ashworths dictate what information they deemed appropriate to share. Perhaps they believed withholding information about Ken or Daddy was in Jolene's best interest.

"I'm sorry to hear about your father. I liked him very much. If I'd known, I'd have gone to his funeral. You know me and papers. Don't even watch the news on television."

"If you're marrying a politician, current events should be a priority."

"Alicia Davenport preps me on talking points before every event."

Dwight snickered. "The Jolene I remember knew her own mind. Since when did you become a verbal puppet?"

Fiddlers Fling

"I wouldn't want to do or say anything to hurt Robert's campaign." She pursed her lips and snarled silently, glad Dwight couldn't see her agitation. "I thought this conversation was about Daddy."

"I know you and Big Mike still aren't on speaking terms. And I wasn't sure if you'd talk to me if I called. But I felt you should know what's going on here."

A sorrow, long suppressed, bucked. Proving she was still a Murdock, anger took over where reason should reign. Hearing Dwight's voice catapulted her into oceans of remorse. How could she go back to Brookside and not be chased by those demons?

She cast her eyes toward the ceiling as if uttering a prayer to Eleanor, and imagined her counsel: *Regret is a dangerous pool to swim in.*

"If what you're telling me is true, how do you think I can be of help? I burned my Brookside bridges when I left my father's house."

"You do whatever you think you have to do. Never met a Murdock that wasn't stubborn through and through."

Apparently time had failed to marinate Dwight Etting into a human being. "I'll choose to ignore that one."

"I get that you're still as angry with me as you are with your father. You need to find a way to get past being mad at us. Big Mike needs you. I need you. The business is suffering. I don't know how much longer we can stay afloat."

Perhaps Dwight's call wasn't motivated by kindness or to convince her marrying a politician was a huge mistake. Nor had he called to woo her back to Brookside and into his arms. He had a lot at stake if Murdock & Etting went down the tubes. However, if Daddy chose to run the business into the ground, that was his choice. He'd turned his back on her a long time ago—as had Dwight. Why should she help either one of them? "Do you expect me to wave a magic wand? Fix Murdock & Etting by a simple *bibbidi bobbidi boo?*"

She should have phrased that last remark a little softer. Still, Dwight Etting didn't deserve courtesy, not after seven years of silence. She'd be the bigger person and extend civility anyway. "I apologize. That last comment was uncalled for. Go on."

After a brief pause, during which she imagined him swallowing the words he'd like to hurl back at her, he continued. "If finances aren't turned around, Murdock & Etting will be bankrupt in three months. I'm powerless to make the changes to stop the disaster. And Big Mike refuses to cooperate."

Daddy's temperament had always been his Achilles Heel, his temper, the fodder for Brookside gossip on more than one occasion. No wonder folks called him "The Fighting Irishman," a moniker he'd worn since boyhood, a trait mellowed by a strong faith.

Did she want to risk her father's rejection a second time? And what of the other demons in Brookside she thought she'd escaped? "I don't mean to sound unsympathetic. I'll see what I can do. Have you talked to the church leaders at Brookside Community? Daddy used to be a deacon."

"He resigned after you left and hasn't set foot in church since. The new pastor, Tim Brentwood, doesn't know much about your father—or Brookside either."

Uncertainty, blame, and remembrance caused her to pace. She wandered into the living room. How was she to blame for decisions Daddy made after she left home? "I don't know what I can do. As for the business, I understand it's important to you, but not to me. If it folds, it folds. I don't need my father's money."

"Not if you're marrying an Ashworth."

Rage trumped her dwindling patience. She tapped *end call* and slam-dunked her cell onto the hated chaise. Dwight had more nerve than a hungry cockroach. She yelled at her iPhone as if he were still listening. "There's nothing I can do. My father disowned me."

Go to him.

She felt her eyes widen. *Is that you, God?*

More than likely the voice in her head was not divine, rather echoes from a migraine wanting to erupt. Still, she felt compelled to respond. *Why should I?*

Because he's your father.

Marrying an Ashworth would not alter the fact Murdock blood ran through her veins. She remembered how Daddy'd knelt at Grandpa's casket, weeping unashamedly though father and son hadn't spoken for two years. "A Murdock might not talk to another Murdock, Jolene, but family is family," Daddy had said. "No argument's strong enough to change that."

Her cell vibrated again, and she picked up. Same Brookside number. Dwight wasn't going to give her any peace.

"If you hang up on me again, I might be forced to come to Albany and stalk you until I've said what needs to be said."

"No need to come to Albany. Say what you have to say."

"You won't like it."

An understatement.

"A lot has happened since you left Brookside, especially after you got engaged to that thief."

"Robert's not a thief."

"Ashworth money is as tainted as FDR's on the Delano side."

"They weren't criminals."

"Their money came from the opium trade."

"It was legal at that time."

"Doesn't make it moral. Pity you can't see the kind of family you're marrying into. Your father knew—the reason he didn't want you to work for them, let alone become one of them."

"More like he gave me an ultimatum."

"I doubt he meant it the way you took it. Big Mike is stubborn, true, but he always had a soft spot for you. If you'd given him half a chance ... "

Dwight's fixation on Ashworth integrity, or lack thereof, was as one-sided as Daddy's feud-like distrust. Jolene readied to end the conversation—again—however, a hitch in Dwight's voice told of more bad news to come. "Your hedging is driving me nuts. There's something else you're not telling me. Talk to me, you coward."

"It's his liver."

"And?"

"Cancer."

Not possible. Not her father. Not the massive man who towered six feet, who played Santa at all the Brookside Christmas functions, his jolly smile, puffy cheeks, long white hair and beard, the trademark photo of Murdock & Etting. Daddy always joked, "Who wouldn't want to do business with a man who could pass as St. Nick's brother?"

"I refuse to believe it. What about a transplant?"

"Too late for that."

"Why didn't the doctor call me?"

"Doc Benson's hands were tied. Big Mike told him not to tell anyone."

"So how do you know?"

"My father found out just before he died. When he started getting calls from creditors, he nosed around your father's correspondence and found medical records with the diagnosis."

Jolene plopped onto the chaise, her body rigid with shock. Daddy was too stubborn to die. "I can't wrap my head around all this."

"I truly didn't want to make this call, but I sensed you didn't know your father was so ill. Otherwise, you'd have come to see him by now. I figure the Ashworths were keeping things from you, and that you had a right to know."

"Robert knows?"

"I assume so. They know everything that happens in Brookside."

Ire built, this time toward Robert. If he knew, why did he keep her father's condition from her? A question she'd pose to him in a few minutes. "And I suppose you hoped I'd drop everything and come to your rescue? Maybe ask my rich fiancé to save Murdock & Etting?"

Dwight half-whispered his response. "Robert Ashworth is the last person I'd ask for help. Like you, my world won't end if Murdock & Etting ceases to exist."

He disconnected.

Jolene rose from the chaise and resumed pacing, an ethereal whisper like an angelic huff in her ear.

He's your father. He's dying. He needs you. Family is family. No argument changes that.

Even if she wanted to play the dutiful daughter, how could she? Daddy made her choose, and she chose Robert. Cancer wouldn't change that. Whatever her father needed, she could manage from afar.

Besides, how could she pick up and leave now? Robert's campaign was in full swing, and her wedding only eight weeks away, a social event that promised to be the biggest Albany had seen in years. Although Mary Ashworth made all the arrangements, down to Jolene's Vera Wang gown, the bride should be available in case anyone cared enough to ask her opinion.

He's your father. He needs you.

She could at the least make a few phone calls, ask the doctor to make a referral to Nursing Services or Adult Protective Services. That's what most social workers would advise their clients' families. Going to Brookside, besides an expenditure of time she could ill afford, would open floodgates she thought dammed for eternity.

She expected Dwight to call again. She checked her messages. Nothing from him, but she should respond to the five missed phone calls from Mother Mary and Robert. If the calls weren't returned soon, they'd probably send in the SWAT team. Jolene switched her phone to ringtone.

It jangled before she could slip it back into her cashmere blazer pocket. She checked the number ... not Dwight. Robert. She let the tune play a few more bars of "Orange Blossom Special." He hated the song, and Mother Mary had demanded Jolene change the ringtone to opera. Sometimes defiance tasted sweet.

"Yes, Robert."

"You didn't respond to my messages. What were you doing?"

"I do have friends, you know. You're not the only one who calls me."

"Then who were you talking to?"

"If you must know, it was Dwight Etting."

Robert laughed—several scales shy of maniacal, yet still chilling. Dwight's name brought as much emotion from Robert as his name evoked in Dwight. "What did he want?"

"Nothing."

"If Dwight Etting called you, he wants something. Money, I'll bet, to save your father's precious company."

Heat surged, and her cheeks burned. "You knew my father was in trouble, knew he was sick and didn't tell me?" *And knew Dwight was back in Brookside?*

"I didn't tell you about your father's cancer because I didn't think you cared."

"I *do* care."

"Look. I'm sorry you found out this way. If I'd known it was important to you, I would have told you."

"I doubt that. Sometimes I think you don't know me at all. You're so wrapped up in politics you can't see me for who I am. You're obsessed with Brookside, and yet you tell me nothing."

"My political survival depends on winning the Brookside Democratic primary. Gordon Brockway, Jr., might be the new Democratic Chair, but your father's opinions still hold weight in the local party. Alicia believes his demeaning remarks are hurting my campaign. Why should I feel sorry for him?"

Jolene swallowed her resentment at the mention of Alicia Davenport. *If murder were only legal.*

"Besides, Dwight Etting seems to share your father's dislike for my family."

Jolene tired of the debate and fell silent. She'd made her decision.

"You're not thinking of going to Brookside, are you?"

"I think I should."

"What about our wedding?"

"What decisions your family lets me make can be handled by phone." She pictured his petulant fingers tapping his mahogany desk.

"I see your mind is already made up. Is this how our marriage is going to be? You gallivanting all over the North Country? You know I want you by my side for campaign events."

"It'll only be for a few days."

"You won't be able to save his business."

"That's not why I'm going."

Robert's *humph* unmasked his impatience. "Why then? To drive me crazy? You do enjoy challenging me at every turn."

Her screech nearly deafened her own ears. "I don't expect you to understand, and I'm angry that you kept his illness from me."

"Mother thought it best not to upset you before the wedding when there was nothing you could do to help him. She meant to be kind."

She lowered her voice back to an acceptable tone. "He's my father."

"No one can help their heritage."

"What does that mean?"

"All I'm saying is you don't owe your father anything. He kicked you out—because of me. He doesn't deserve your loyalty."

"What if your father were dying?"

"He's not. He jogs four miles every day."

She hadn't cried since she left Brookside, and today would be no exception. Tears did nothing to sway Robert, and she needed his empathy, not his twisted logic. "Have you no heart?"

"Not for a man who mistreated the woman I'm going to marry."

Fiddlers Fling

How typical of Robert to smother a declaration of love with condemnation. Robert had his faults, but no one was perfect. "I might be angry," she said, "but I still love you."

She didn't expect him to return sentiment—not his style. His *tsk*, however, roared like a crashing avalanche. "If you must go, stay at the family estate. I'll let Alicia know so she can keep tabs on the paparazzi. Drive carefully. Call me when you get there."

She disconnected.

Jolene threw in one more change of clothes and set Eleanor Roosevelt's biography in a protective pouch before closing the suitcase. Glad for rollers, she marveled at the weight—more cosmetics than clothes.

The doorbell surprised her. Living in the attached guest quarters, she rarely had unannounced visitors.

"Who is it?" she asked through the intercom.

"It's Mother Mary."

Jolene opened the door, and her future mother-in-law marched in, quickly owning the living room. "So it's true. You're going to Brookside. Your father may be ill, but he threw you out. We're your family now."

"He's dying."

"I applaud your sentimentality, Jolene, the very thing that makes you a top-notch social worker. But use common sense, my dear. You can handle anything your father needs from here. And if needed, we'll pay for his home care. You must realize that running off to Brookside so near the wedding is totally irresponsible."

Jolene felt her knees wobble. Robert eventually caved to her wishes if she stood her ground long enough. Yet, she cowered in the presence of the Ashworth matriarch, as abominable as a Yeti, as ruthless as she was generous. Not that Jolene wanted to go against Mother Mary's wishes. The woman was more than a mentor, and her counsel almost always included the salt of reason. Not today. An Ashworth couldn't possibly comprehend Murdock loyalty, written into Jolene's genetic makeup. "Family is family. I have to go. I don't expect you, Sean, or even Robert, to approve, let alone understand."

Mother Mary scowled, wrinkling her hundred-dollar facial. "You're right. I neither understand nor approve. You're setting yourself up for more disappointment."

"That's my choice to make."

"If you're so determined to set out on a fool's errand, at least promise me you'll stay at our family home—for your protection."

"What on earth would I need protection from in Brookside?"

"Our enemies are everywhere. Now that you're engaged to Robert, you're a target as well."

Jolene had never been inside the centuries-old fortress belonging to Brookside's First Family, a historical landmark that adorned the crest of Gnome Mountain, its splendor the talk of tourists, its magnificence the stuff of legend. Now she'd stay as the heir's intended, an honored guest.

"Promise me you won't stick me with a bodyguard."

"Very well. But check in often."

She'd accept, not from obedience but from curiosity. Would the place be as garish as all the other Ashworth estates?

Chapter Two

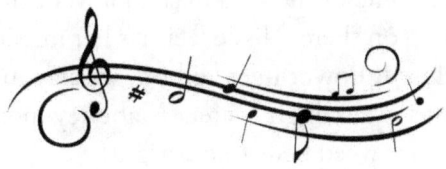

Dwight cast his line into Weinstein's Inlet, so named after the moonshiner who once lived in the abandoned shack at the top of the knoll and supposedly met his end in a drunken fall into the stream that fed the pond.

His foreman and Army buddy, Jack Mahoney, put another worm on his hook and recast. "Fish better bite today. I haven't caught anything out of this spot in two weeks."

"Used to be filled with bass until Ashworth built the chemical plant upstream."

"Let's try wading out a bit. Looks as though the bass have pretty much eaten the weed beds near shore."

"Can't do any worse." Dwight went to the truck and returned with their hip boots. "For a city boy, you seem to know a lot about nature. Weren't that many fishing holes in Afghanistan. The way you could shoot a soda can off a rooftop, I figured you more for a hunter."

"I hated being a sniper, and I'm glad to have put the uniform aside. Doubly glad you asked me to move out here. Chicago got on my nerves. Doc thought the rat-a-tat, sirens, and noises triggered PTSD. Since I moved here, I'm doing better."

"I'm not so sure I did you a favor. If business doesn't pick up, you might be the next man I lay off. With a wife, and a kid on the way, I won't blame you if you try to find something more lucrative, even if it means moving back to the city."

"Country living is just what this war-weary veteran needs. Besides, Nissie expects to go back to work for the DA after maternity leave. We won't starve."

"So, she really likes her job?"

"Yeah. She can't share all the particulars, but she's helping him with a fraud case on a women's clinic in Bakersfield."

"Fremont Clinic?"

"Yeah."

"I've heard of it. Some of the girls in school went there for abortions."

"Shady stuff going on there. Nissie feels it's her mission to help her boss build evidence to close it down. I get laid off, we stay in Brookside."

They waded into waist-high water. Mahoney pointed to a nearby shallow area. "There are weed beds to our right."

Dwight worried that Mahoney's so-called PTSD had been a sacrificial ruse, giving up a thriving carpentry business to help a friend. Before he could decide whether or not to mention if such were the case, Mahoney continued.

"Quit beating yourself up over my decision to come out here. I did it for my family. Fresh air ... " He glanced toward the chemical plant. "Well ... mostly ... good people ... we're happy here. God will provide."

"What will you do if the business caves?"

"I've got my music. Our band always has room for a keyboardist if you want to join us."

"Thanks."

If Jolene couldn't get her father to sign the new contracts, he might have to take Mahoney up on that offer or move away. Brookside was a great place to raise a family, but Dwight's prospects of having one seemed more distant than ever.

Ten years Dwight's senior, fifty pounds lighter and three inches shorter, Mahoney moved through the water as if born to the stream. Weinstein's Inlet held no challenge for a man who worked hard at keeping fit.

Dwight shook his head. He'd been out of the Army only a year, and already he was twenty pounds heavier than his discharge weight. Mahoney hadn't been out long enough for his hair to grow past his ears, but long enough to start a beard contest—and he was winning. He made a contest of everything, especially work-related tasks, betting who could paint a garage the fastest. As if reading Dwight's mind, Mahoney proposed a wager. "First to catch a legal, edible fish buys lunch." He signaled toward a school of bass on the other side of the weed bed. The men recast.

Dwight got the first nibble. Soon his line tugged. "It's a big one. I don't suppose you brought the net."

Mahoney smiled. "Let's see a country boy get that bass the old-fashioned way."

Dwight worked the line and reached for the club in his belt when Mahoney's phone chimed the melody for "Chicago, Chicago, My Kind of Town."

Dwight dropped his hold on the bass, which slid back into the water and swam away.

"Seriously, Mahoney? You didn't leave the phone on dry ground? What if you'd tripped?"

"I didn't, did I? It's Nissie." He slid the icon over. "What's up? You okay?"

Listening intently, his smirk meant Nissie, the real head of the household, had a proposition of her own. "Got it. Extra cheese. Don't forget the pineapple, ham, and anchovies." He blew his cheeks out as if in disgust as he pocketed his cell.

"Got to go. Wife wants pizza. No one warned me how demanding a woman can be so close to her due date. Be glad when this little one arrives and life gets back to normal."

"I may not have a kid, but I'm pretty sure your life will never be like it was before Nissie got pregnant. Man up, my friend."

"Did I tell you we're having a boy?"

"Only eight times."

They waded to shore, took off their boots, secured their lines, and put the gear into the truck. Dwight took out his flip-phone from the glove compartment and scrolled for messages.

"When you going to get a real phone?"

"Nothing wrong with this one."

"Can't even buy 'em any longer."

"What do I need with all those apps?"

"You and technology have always been strangers. I swear you're living in a time bubble that carried you here from the nineteenth century. Did you even bother to read the email I sent you yesterday?"

"Haven't been on the computer in a few days."

"Figures. You use the dang thing so little it's not even worth the monthly internet charge if you ask me."

Dwight's laugh echoed over the stream. "I'm not asking. Besides, your emails are usually invites for a blind date."

"Can't blame a friend for trying, man."

"Why is it you married men can't stand to see a happy bachelor?"

"Oh, I could stand it if you were happy. You haven't had a date since you broke up with Alicia Davenport. What happened?"

"Every other sentence was about Robert Ashworth's senatorial bid and how I should work at the local campaign headquarters with her. I was a target, not a boyfriend."

"Still ... a shame. Wouldn't mind a bit if that girl broke into my dreams. What a looker."

They slid into Dwight's truck and sped toward Antonio's Pizzeria. Shouldn't keep a pregnant woman's craving unsatisfied for very long.

Mahoney put his hands behind his head as he leaned back. "Heard from Jolene?"

Dwight sneaked a quick peek at Mahoney before returning his eyes to the road. "She's coming this afternoon."

"I tell you, Dwight, it's a mistake to involve her. She'll bring the wrath of the Ashworths with her. There's got to be some other way." He grinned. "I saw you reading a text on your wannabe phone about a hundred times. Any chance it was from Jolene?"

"Wants me to meet her at the Main Street Café."

Mahoney laughed. "Doesn't she know Ashworth tore it down last year and turned the place into a Gentleman's Club?"

"Apparently she's pretty ignorant about what happens in Brookside. I suspect the Ashworths prefer it that way. If I say something to try to open her eyes, she gets defensive. She has her reasons for standing by her fiancé. I should try to respect that."

Dwight pulled into Antonio's parking lot. "I'll wait here while you get Nissie's pizza."

Mahoney nodded and slid out. "Won't be long."

Leaning back against the headrest, Dwight closed his eyes, but his thoughts whirled. Maybe Jolene's ignorance about all things Brookside was more by choice than Ashworth manipulation. The less she knew, the less likely she'd be lured back home. How often he'd hoped she'd come to her senses. Leave Albany and return to her roots. Her svelte form loomed on the river banks of his memory—her sparkling blue eyes that danced when angry, blonde curls that draped slender shoulders, a prom queen with a tilted crown—casual perfection the ilk of her sensuality.

Big Mike had no recent family pictures at the office or at his house, and Dwight hadn't seen Jolene in three years. Would her smile still take his breath away? Judging from their earlier brief conversation, she'd probably never smile at him again.

He opened his eyes and sat up to send Jolene a reply text—Main Street Café out of business. Meet at Big Mike's.

Mahoney came back into the truck and balanced Nissie's pizza on his lap. "Reading that text again, I see. You're a man obsessed."

"Just sending a reply. Going to meet her at Big Mike's."

"Whoa! And you think there're fireworks on the Fourth of July? Isn't that a bit risky?"

"I know. Big Mike's apt to push me out the door one step behind Jolene. But those two need to face one another again. I'll provide the opportunity and let God do the rest."

"Man sure has a temper."

"With a heart to match. Did I ever tell you how Murdock & Etting came to be?"

Mahoney took a sip from his soda can. "Actually, no. I always wondered."

"This town was once a thriving place. The largest employer was Eastman's Outerwear, a factory specializing in sporting attire. Had an outlet store attached. People came from miles. When Eastman went bankrupt, Ashworth Enterprises bought the factory and turned it into offices. A lot of men went on unemployment with few prospects for another job. That year, a drought put a lot of farms out of business, my father's included. Ashworth bought up most of the land. Big Mike started this company to give men like my father hope, a chance to start over. I owe him. Brookside owes him."

"And you seriously think Jolene will turn patriot against the royal Ashworths?"

"A man can dream, can't he?"

Chapter Three

Dwight mused on the drive to Big Mike's. Would this prove to be the mistake Mahoney predicted? What if Big Mike wouldn't let him in? Some days he didn't. And some days, he could barely navigate. Other days the man showed no evidence of physical limitations—a congenial mood and agility hitting the upper scale of efficiency. *Lord, let today be one of those days.*

Dwight loved the man like a second father. In his youth, the Murdock home had bulged with pick-up bands and practices for area music contests, Dwight's keyboard and guitar added into the mix. He missed the music—playing with Jolene and Big Mike, best fiddlers in the North Country.

Did she still play?

Most of all, Dwight remembered Jolene's rendition of *Amazing Grace.* When the bullets ricocheted off Afghan huts, he imagined her staccato plucks and fantasized about coming home to Jolene—falling into a war hero's arms.

Dwight hesitated at the door, then knocked four times. No answer. Television noises blared from inside. Either Big Mike had fallen asleep or he simply refused to get up from his chair unless the neighbor came over with a home-cooked supper. Dwight tried the handle, and the heavy glass door swung open.

"Big Mike? It's Dwight."

No response. He peeked into the den. Big Mike slumped in the plaid winged chair while *The Price is Right* bonged so loud the room shook. A shotgun rested across his lap.

Was he dead? Would God let that happen before Jolene got right with her father? Loud snorts put an end to dread. Perhaps he should leave, come back in an hour or so. Then Big Mike jumped from his chair.

"Who's there?"

"It's Dwight."

"Dwight who?"

Up until now, Big Mike recognized most people, although he'd forgotten the names of the newest work crew. Dwight imagined the man's intermittent and momentary memory lapses to be more the result of too much beer than from cancer.

"Dwight Etting."

Big Mike whirled, the shotgun held straight out with seeming intent to fire.

"Whoa—"

"Got ya!" He laughed and put the rifle down. "I still know my mind, Dwight. Take a seat, boy. Why ain't you at the office today?"

Jolene would have her hands full. First on the agenda should be to clear the house of weapons. Next, booze.

"It's Saturday. We don't work unless we're on a tight schedule."

"I know that. Love to mess with you, Dwight. You're too easy. To what do I owe the pleasure?"

Big Mike never missed an opportunity to mess with Dwight's head ... his second favorite pastime after playing the fiddle. Maybe if the man picked it up again, he'd stop scaring his protégé half to death. Dwight scanned the once-hefty Brookside legend, now an emaciated portrait of the Big Mike Dwight knew growing up. Dwight sat down on the sofa and picked up the remote. "Okay if I turn off the television?"

Big Mike sat back down. "Sounds serious."

"It is."

"Give it to me straight. Like I always say, rip the bandage off. If I have a heart attack, well, cuts short the cancer."

"Jolene is coming home."

Big Mike's smile faded. "When?"

"She's meeting me here in an hour."

"Kind of springing it on me."

"Thought it best that way."

"Suppose you're right. If you told me yesterday, I might have changed the locks."

Dwight caught the sight of three empty beer bottles on the tray next to Big Mike's chair, the yeast blast indicating they'd been opened recently. Big Mike faced challenges head-on. A mystery why he reverted to a lifestyle he'd abandoned thirty years ago. He'd coped with a wife's death, losing his farm, and nearly losing the construction company in the last recession. Maybe Jolene's desertion was the proverbial straw.

"I don't want to see her."

"Someone's got to look after you."

"I don't need no looking after. I'm doing just fine."

Dwight picked up a beer bottle and waved it at Big Mike. "Yeah, so I see. When was the last time you had something to eat today besides barley?"

"Don't recall, but I'm sure I had breakfast. Louise came over earlier and put some food in the refrigerator."

"If it weren't for the goodness of your neighbor, you'd probably starve. Let me get you some lunch."

"I can get it for myself."

"Well, I haven't eaten, and I promised to meet Jolene here."

"Help yourself to whatever you find."

"Don't want to eat alone. Sure you won't join me?"

"Guess I could eat a little something."

Dwight took out the leftover egg casserole, put a couple of ham slices on top of the dish, and heated the food in the microwave. He washed out the microwave with a paper towel and tossed it in the garbage can on top of the blackened bananas and moldy bread. Louise must have cleaned the cupboards again.

Big Mike lumbered into the kitchen, his gait not as spry as a few weeks ago, but steady.

"Nothing like the smell of ham to stir up an appetite."

"You worry me, Mike. You need to eat more regularly."

"That's what Louise says."

"She's the salt of the earth."

"Good cook." Big Mike winked. "And good company. She carts me around in her car too. Doc doesn't want me driving. I'd drive anyway, but this way Louise comes over more."

Fiddlers Fling

Dwight paused his search for cooking utensils and fixed his eyes on Big Mike. "Why, you old hound dog, you."

The man's eyes twinkled, but he didn't respond. "Louise brought over a couple of spatulas and put them in the drawer right of the sink." When Dwight was last here, Big Mike had no dishes, silverware, or even paper products. "Got anything to put this food on, or are we just going to eat like cavemen?"

"Louise keeps sending over paper plates and plasticware. I got a whole pantry full."

Dwight dished up the food, then set the plates on the table.

Big Mike gobbled his eggs in three bites. He attempted to slice the ham, but the plastic knife snapped in two. He picked the meat up and ate the ham like a slice of bread. "More than one way to chow down ham."

"Maybe Louise would take you to the store to buy dishes. What happened to everything, anyway?"

Instead of answering, Big Mike picked up his plate and threw it in the trash. "Jolene really coming?"

"Wouldn't joke about a thing like that, Mike."

"To stay? Did she finally tell Ashworth to take a hike?"

If only she would. "I won't lie to you. She still plans on marrying the scumbag." Besides an appreciation of country music, the men possessed only two other things in common—a deep love for Jolene and distrust of anyone named Ashworth.

"I take it you don't like the man any more than I do."

Dwight moaned—a Holy Spirit conviction sigh, he was sure. Animosity displeased the Lord. Yet ... well ... even God must find Robert Ashworth despicable. "Let's say, I have to pray a lot not to hate him."

"Well, I stopped praying a long time ago."

"When Jolene left?"

No answer.

"Why'd she leave?"

"We had words."

"You didn't hear from her again?"

His jaw clenched. "She called to tell me she was marrying Sean Ashworth's son. Worst news a father can get. I hung up on her. I know I shouldn't have, but she knows I can't stand hearing the name. What did she expect? She can come home if she wants. This is her house ... will be soon enough, anyways. Don't mean I have to talk to her."

Dwight knew that forgiveness came hard for a man like Big Mike Murdock. Back in the day, his rigidity was more like unbendable heroism, the stuff that made him a formidable opponent against Ashworth greed.

Jolene didn't fall far from the Murdock apple tree.

Dwight glanced at his watch. "Before your daughter gets here, we need to talk about the business."

"Don't give a hoot, Dwight."

He found that hard to believe. A man who so tirelessly and passionately built a construction empire to keep a hundred men employed didn't stop caring overnight. "Before he died, Dad said each of you set up durable powers of attorney. Dad named me, and you named Jolene."

"That's right."

"Why Jolene if the two of you weren't speaking?"

"Hope runs eternal, they say. Thought she'd eventually come to her senses. Now she'll probably give everything to Ashworth when I die. Ain't that a kick? I'd sooner go bankrupt. But I suppose there's nothin' I can do about it now."

"The durable part of the power of attorney only means you can't change it if your mental state deteriorates. Far as I can see, you still have your wits, though you're starting to get a little forgetful."

"I remember what's important. What's the point of remembering things I don't need to remember? As for the power of attorney, I won't change it. Jolene gets the whole shebang. I won't disinherit my only kin, even if I go to the grave with her still mad at me. Family's family. But if the business goes, at least Ashworth won't get much. If Jolene's married to an Ashworth, she won't want for anything." Big Mike sneered. "Odd comfort in that."

Dwight groaned. How do you save a drowning man who refuses to grab hold of a life preserver?

Chapter Four

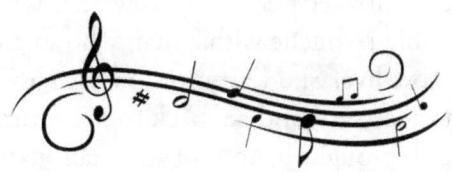

Jolene's BMW bumped the entire quarter-mile driveway to the Murdock homestead. She parked behind a new Ford Ranger, assuming it belonged to Dwight and glad he'd arrived ahead of her as promised. Did Daddy still drive his old Dodge Rambler? He'd never bought a new car since she could remember.

She glanced at the familiar row of lilacs next to the barn, untrimmed but full and vibrant. Spring often came late to the North Country—this year later than normal. Years past, with the first buds, she and her father would haul out the ATVs.

Did he still own them?

She rushed out of the car and hurried to the barn window, disappointed when the crusted layer of dirt prevented a view of the interior. She made her way to the sliding door. Padlocked. Crazy to hope the Raptor was still there. She last rode the day before she left Brookside.

Although Daddy had owned snowmobiles, she liked the ATVs best, speeding over dirt roads with Dwight, sneaking a few kisses—sometimes more than a few. Dwight had been a good kisser, with strong arms and broad shoulders, but a boy without ambition, destined to mediocrity, according to Mary Ashworth.

Curiosity spiked, and she checked in the backyard and peeked under the tarp. Daddy's Summit. Somewhere in her child's heart, she'd hoped against hope he'd kept her Raptor, a chance to take one last wild ride before settling in as a demure senator's wife. One last rebellion.

Fiddlers Fling

She turned her gaze toward the dingy white farmhouse, the missing chunks of clapboard yet to be replaced after the blizzard of '93. Daddy always promised he'd get to it, but never found the time or the money.

He'd joke how the plumber's house sported leaky pipes, and the carpenter's house was kept together with glue and strategically placed nails. As a child, she never gave an old barn or dilapidated house a second thought.

Love lived inside then.

The exterior decay mirrored her feelings toward this hopeless mission, to think she could possibly reconcile with a man who so completely despised the life she would now live. She'd arrange for her father's long-term care needs, whatever was necessary, and get back to her future in Albany.

The snap of a limb brought her out of self-examination. She turned. A middle-aged woman, perhaps early fifties, approached. She held a freshly baked apple pie in one hand and a stack of paper plates in the other. "May, I help you, dear?"

"Who are you?" Jolene asked.

"I was about to ask you the same question. If you must know, my name is Louise Fournier. I rent the farmhouse down the road. I'm a friend of Mr. Murdock."

"I'm Big Mike's daughter, Jolene."

"Oh, I didn't know Michael had a daughter!"

Jolene arched a brow. Michael? Everyone in Brookside called her father, Big Mike.

"I assumed he was a lonely widower. When I heard he was so sick, I thought it my Christian duty to check up on him. Afraid he'd starve otherwise. Listen to me ramble on. Goodness gracious, dear, you should get in before it rains again."

Slightly obese, with a round face framed by wispy salt-and-pepper hair and twinkling eyes that probably veered toward the mischievous in her younger years, she apparently wasn't from Brookside or she'd have known Jolene—if not by appearance, at least by name.

"I was just about to knock."

"Needn't bother. I have a key." She tried the door. "Never mind. It's already open, I see. Must be Dwight's here."

They entered. A more mature, filled-out version of Jolene's high school boyfriend sat at the kitchen table. He met her gaze with the same mesmerizing, coconut eyes she remembered. "Jolene. Hello, Louise. Didn't know you'd be back again. Big Mike said you were here earlier with a breakfast casserole."

She put the pie on the table. "Don't normally come over more than once on the weekend," she said to Jolene. "Dwight and his friend stop by on Saturday and Sunday. Since I had to bake for tomorrow's church supper, I made an extra pie for Michael. Where is he?"

"In the den," Dwight said.

"*Family Feud* again?" Louise glanced toward Jolene. "Never saw a man so mired into television. If he ain't watching the *Game Show Network*, he's all about the *History Channel*, particularly those *American Picker* shows."

Dwight opened a cupboard drawer, apparently as familiar in this house as in his own, retrieved a pie server, then sliced Louise's offering. "I'll bring him in a piece. He just had lunch."

"Figures," Louise said. "It's half past two. Man won't eat unless somebody stays and eats with him."

Dwight put a big slice of pie on a paper plate while Louise walked to the archway, peeked into the den, then came back to the kitchen. "Dwight, you're gonna have to get him to put the shotgun away before he shoots somebody."

Dwight laughed. "Nearly shot me earlier. Though he says he was only joking. I'll see what I can do."

Jolene gasped. *Shotgun?* She glanced back and forth. Dwight and Louise's banter sounded like old housewives swapping stories over the backyard fence. Dwight left with Daddy's pie, leaving Jolene quite confused as to the woman's charitable activities toward her father.

"Where are my manners? Dear, would you like a slice? I know Dwight loves my pie as much as your father, so I didn't have to ask."

"If you and Dwight are having a piece, I'll join you."

Louise promptly cut three more slices and plopped them onto paper plates. "Won't likely find a clean fork. I keep Michael supplied with plastic since he's loathe to wash a dish."

At one time, Jolene had been as familiar with the kitchen as Dwight and Louise. Now she felt like a stranger. She opened the pantry door and handed Louise the plastic utensils. "Thank you for your kindness to my father. I'm grateful Daddy has friends like you and Dwight to look in on him."

Fiddlers Fling

Louise offered a broad smile. "Oh, I don't do much. Your father hardly lets me do any housework. I occasionally sneak a load of laundry over to my place. Otherwise, Michael would wear the same clothes 'til the second coming. Sometimes bribery works. 'Michael,' I say, 'I'm making a tuna sandwich. It'll be ready for you as soon as you get out of the shower.' Doesn't work all the time. Man has a stubborn streak a mile long. He accepts my cooking, and we go out for a ride now and again. He won't let me do much else. I don't force the matter. Let him make his own decisions. This morning, I managed to clean out the spoiled stuff. Funny how he always throws his paper plates away, but won't part with moldy bread."

If the rest of the house looked like the kitchen floor, a good cleaning was in order. Jolene bit her lip when she saw the pile of beer bottles in the garbage. Daddy never drank that she knew of. Though some of the older folks in town used to say he'd been a hellion, a description she later learned that meant a hard-living man, before he met her mother.

Jolene spoke up. "I know how important it is to respect a person's need for independence. I'm a social worker."

"You are? Say ... you do look a mite familiar. Where have I seen you before?"

"I'm engaged to Robert Ashworth. You may have seen our picture in the paper. The Ashworths are Brookside residents but spend half their time in Albany where Robert's father runs a law firm."

"Oh, yes. I do recall, now. I'm not from here, as you probably guessed. I hail from Burlington, Vermont. My husband was a lot older, and we moved here after he retired, going on two years ago. My Henry died six months after we moved."

"I'm sorry."

"No need to be. We had a good life together. Lots of memories. No children, though. I liked the peace and quiet here, so I decided to stay on after he passed." She handed Jolene a plate.

Dwight came back in and grabbed his slice of goodness. "Big Mike wants me to tell you you make the best pie he's ever eaten."

Daddy used to claim his daughter made the best apple pie in the North Country. Was Louise's better? Jolene took a bite. *No.* She'd be sure to make her father an apple pie before she returned to Albany— perhaps jar his memory as to whose pie took the prize.

Dwight gulped his slice in three bites like Daddy used to do. "Umm.

Delicious, as always, Louise. Thanks for stopping by."

"Well, I see you two know each other, and I have laundry to switch from the washer to the dryer." She wrote a phone number on a piece of napkin and gave it to Jolene. "Call me if you need anything. I'm just a holler away."

"You walked up that long driveway?"

"Our properties abut. I go across the field."

"That's Ken Etting's house. Are you Dwight's relative?"

Dwight smiled and answered for her. "No. A tenant."

Jolene expected Brookside wouldn't be the same. Yet, that someone else besides an Etting lived next door didn't seem right. "Where are you living, Dwight?"

"In the apartment over the office."

Louise headed toward the door. "Dwight's the best landlord a widow like me could ask for." With that, she was gone.

Jolene looked at Dwight. "Nice woman."

"Louise is the best." He gazed at Jolene like a man eyes steak and potatoes. "Well, well, well. The future Mrs. Robert Ashworth, sharing a piece of pie with a lowly carpenter. I can't believe you're here." His smile tilted to one side, half sneer and half frown.

"I never break a promise. Unlike some people, I know."

"I thought we were going to forget prom night. We were foolish kids."

"I can't. Sorry."

"Why not?"

"Because ... I don't know. Maybe because I never saw you again until now?"

"You saw me when we graduated, and when I came home on leave."

"You know what I mean. Why won't Daddy come into the kitchen? I'd like to talk to him."

Dwight sat on a stool by the counter. "He said you could come here if you wanted, but that didn't mean he had to talk to you. He took the main staircase up to his room. Give him time."

"At least he didn't throw me out."

Dwight handed Jolene his key. "Jack has one, too. I'll get a duplicate made from his."

"Jack?"

Fiddlers Fling

"Our foreman, a friend of mine from Afghanistan. Good man. His wife's expecting a baby any day."

A chill raced up her spine. *Baby*. She'd like to be a mother someday, but she didn't deserve a family.

Jolene pocketed the key.

"Big Mike says you can stay as long as you want. It's your house as much as it is his. See, he does care. Just won't admit it. Haven't met a Murdock wasn't stubborn through and through."

Jolene pulled out a kitchen chair and sat. "Ouch."

"I'm just sayin' ... " His face wore tension as if a tremendous weight pulled at his once beautiful smile. "Thing is, if neither one of you bends, you'll both break." He grabbed his denim jacket from the peg bar by the back door, a faint smile erupting. "Any plans for supper?"

"Not yet. It's only four."

"Well, there's not much food in this house except Louise's leftovers. If you want, you can come over to my place. I cook a mean hamburger. I'll take you shopping for groceries after we eat."

"I'm staying at the Ashworth Estate, so I don't need food for myself. I suppose I should get supplies for my father." She might not want to know the answer but asked anyway. "Why the apartment, Dwight? Why aren't you living in your old house?"

He adjusted his hunting cap. "When things started going down the tubes, my father rented our house and moved to the apartment, so he'd have a few dollars to put back into the business."

"What about the lot on the other side of town where the cabin was? Did he rent that out too?"

"He sold it just before he died."

"Who bought it?"

"Who do you think?"

"If I knew, I wouldn't ask."

"Ashworth, of course."

"That's a valuable piece of property. A beautiful view of the river."

"Ashworth plans to build a strip mall there."

Robert should have told her. If not him, Mary or Sean. Although, to be fair, when she first went to work for them, she'd made it clear she wanted to be kept out of business matters, that all she cared about was the Foundation.

"A strip mall would change the whole landscape of that part of Brookside. I thought it was zoned as residential."

"Zoning laws are easy to change when you own half the town and bribe the other half."

Sean Ashworth had always been a shrewd businessman, but only Dwight and Daddy accused him of indecency.

"Robert has little to do with the family business apart from the law firm."

"The apple doesn't fall far from the tree, Jolene."

"Even if what you say about Sean is true, not every greedy parent spawns bad fruit. Robert believes each man needs to stand accountable for his own actions, not that of his ancestors. He's not the monster you make him out to be. Do you really think I'd marry him if he were?"

Dwight bit his lower lip as he muttered, "Vines are pretty to look at, but they strangle everything around them."

"That's a deep thought coming from a boy who refused to read beyond English class requirements."

"Maybe Afghanistan changed the way I look at life."

Jolene tugged at her leather handbag. "You're wrong to judge Robert solely on the basis of his being an Ashworth."

"Maybe so. Or maybe instinct tells me Robert's not the good person you think him to be."

The conversation ping-ponged fresh arguments, as intense as yesterday's phone calls. If she were going to work with Dwight to help her father's business and figure out his care, she'd have to find a way to avoid these verbal jousts. "I'll take you up on your dinner offer on one condition."

"And that is?"

"No more bad-mouthing my fiancé or his family."

Dwight gestured surrender. "A truce ?"

Probably the closest they'd get to a lasting peace. An Etting never apologized. Neither did a Murdock.

Chapter Five

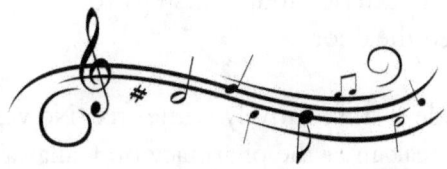

Dwight turned on the truck radio. He might as well let music fill the silence since neither of them seemed willing to start a conversation. He supposed Jolene's shock over her father's health and the near cataclysmic argument at the house must have numbed her. Miracle she didn't get back into her car and head right back Albany right then and there. He would try to avoid trigger words while with her. His dislike of Robert didn't give him the right to be judgmental, at least not to her face. Did she love the man ... or what the Ashworths could do for her? People change and sometimes for the worse. Had she become as shallow as Alicia Davenport?

As those thoughts rolled through his head, the radio played an upbeat version of "We Believe." Apparently it caught Jolene's attention.

"Christian Rock?" she asked, glaring at the dashboard.

"Do you want me to change the station?"

"No, I like it. I listen to the station on occasion when I'm alone. I don't often get the chance. I'm either at Robert's house or off somewhere with Mother Mary for this luncheon or that."

"Mother Mary? You make her sound like a nun."

"It's what she wants me to call her since Robert and I became engaged. I suppose, though, in some ways, she did save me."

"And not the Lord?"

She didn't respond.

"So you don't go to church?"

Fiddlers Fling

"Not very often. Robert and I go on occasion, usually for increased visibility, to swing the Christian voting bloc."

Dwight parked and went to the other side of the truck to help Jolene out. She pushed him away. "I'm not helpless."

With four-inch spikes? Her short legs barely reached the runner. She slid down, and her skirt inched up, revealing slender thighs as she wriggled out of the truck. She straightened her clothes, unabashed by temporary immodesty caused by the struggle to prove her independence.

They climbed the exterior fourteen steps to the apartment entrance, then Dwight opened the door.

"Not locked?"

"Why? Brookside is still relatively crime-free. No vagrants. Although I heard there was a break-in at the pharmacy on Callaway Street. Bunch of kids stole cigarettes and condoms. I don't keep either here."

Jolene giggled—nearly a hearty belly laugh.

"Can I take your jacket?" he asked.

"Yes, you *may*."

"Still correcting my grammar, I see."

She slipped off a black blazer sporting as many brass buttons as a five-star general's full dress uniform and probably costing a small fortune. Her whole attire smacked of *Elle* or *Vogue*, not that he read them, but Alicia did, and Jolene's red fluffy skirt resembled something Alicia would wear.

Dwight carefully laid the coat over the couch, then opted to hang it up since he hadn't vacuumed in over a week. When Jolene shot him a puzzled look, he shrugged. "Sandy sleeps here."

She gifted him with a broad smile. "Sandy? Something tells me she's a lab. Like the one you had in high school."

"You guessed it. I miss Goldie."

"What happened to her?"

"She died while I was in Afghanistan."

Her sympathetic gaze met his. "Seems you've lost a lot over the years. Your dad and your dog. I'm sorry if I've acted like a spoiled brat."

An apology? From Jolene Murdock? Well, miracles did happen after all. "It's okay. Didn't lose everything. Got my religion back during my second deployment."

She cocked her head and pursed her lips, releasing them with a smack. "Good ... I guess. I lost interest a long time ago. After the prom." Her tone rebirthed animosity.

He never should have walked out on her that night. For weeks after, he'd rehearsed a dozen ways to tell her so, but before he actually spoke the words, he was on a bus to Fort Jackson. By now, even a Murdock would have buried the incident into the muck of stupid adolescence. Why did Jolene wear her resentment like a chip on narrow shoulders?

No use dwelling on an imponderable. "Still like dogs?"

"I do. Sometimes I think about getting a pet. Robert won't hear of it. He hates animals ... especially dogs."

One more thing Robert denied her. Seems if a man loved a woman, he'd find pleasure in the things she loved. Dwight sighed. Then again, he hadn't been very thoughtful of her in the past. Had the years made him wiser? He'd like to think so. If given the chance, he'd show her how a man *should* treat a woman. The Jolene he shared childhood with used to play Frisbee with him and Goldie. A shame she'd let the Ashworths suck her spirit dry.

Dwight opened his bedroom door, and Sandy waggled into the living room, smothering him with dog kisses. He glanced toward Jolene, who scowled until Sandy put her head on his guest's lap, her way of welcome. Surprisingly, Jolene didn't push the dog off her expensive skirt—instead she nuzzled Sandy with gusto.

"I should take her out for a bit. Want to walk with us?"

She rubbed Sandy's back and sides. "Sure."

They walked along paths she'd traversed a thousand times in years gone by. Sandy chased the lengthening shadows as the late afternoon sun played hide-and-seek with the clouds. Refreshing breezes, purged by the earlier downpour, carried an aroma like peppermint sprinkled over vanilla ice-cream. Memories flashed again, this time of a late- winter storm a few weeks before prom, and a kiss by the fireplace, a night of passion that got the best of them. Dwight had promised he'd love her forever. He did ... until prom night.

Some say young love never dies. Yet, a river of regret flowed through the last seven years. She'd noticed Dwight's family Bible mounted prominently on his desk. He claimed to have revisited that "Joy, Joy, Joy" of Sunday school song.

Maybe she'd return to church when she and Robert married. He talked the talk and made campaign promises to return prayer to the classroom. Yet, she couldn't recall one Sunday he'd gone to church simply to worship. Tomorrow was Sunday. No reason not to restart an old tradition, with or without Robert.

Out of shape, she wheezed with each of Dwight's long strides. "Slow down. I can't walk as fast as you in these heels." She bent down and took them off, swinging them like a picnic basket in her hand.

He paused. She remembered hours of cross-country skiing in the woods when Dwight would dash ahead, then wait for her to catch up. She hadn't realized how much she missed being outdoors. A childlike urge seized her. Dropping her shoes, she scooped up a handful of wet leaves and shoved them down Dwight's shirt.

"Why, you little ... "

His expected retaliation prolonged the war, a whole-scale mud fight with Sandy chasing their misfires. Laughter energized her, abandonment and frivolity a rare experience these hectic days on Robert's campaign trail.

Spent, even Sandy panting for breath, Jolene put her shoes back on, and they walked back to the apartment. Jolene hadn't realized how stained her clothes were until she caught her reflection in Dwight's living-room mirror.

"Looks as though you ruined your pretty skirt."

"I probably should go shopping for different clothes than what I brought. I didn't pack jeans, either."

"Why not? This is Brookside, the flannel capital of New York State."

"I only have True Religion."

"Excuse me?"

She laughed. "A jeans brand. Two-hundred dollars a pair."

"I'd loan you mine, but I doubt they'd fit."

She surveyed his six-foot frame, muscular arms, and firm chest. "No, I suppose not. Would you mind making an extra stop at ... ?" Her voice trailed off before she continued. "It's been so long. Is Dinty's Dry Goods still around?"

"Most of the Mom-and-Pop stores have been bought out or torn down. There's a strip mall next to the food market. You might find something at Seconds 'R Us. I'll take you there before we grocery shop."

"Sounds doable."

They dined on greasy hamburgers and a side salad, then climbed into Dwight's truck. Surprisingly, he came into the store with her. "Thanks for the company. I thought men hated shopping."

"Most men do. I don't. I confess ... it gives me a chance to study people."

"Why? Are you voyeuristic?"

"Not in the perverted way. Observing human nature makes me a better writer."

Jolene gave him a gentle shove. "Get out of here. You like to write? Since when?"

"Been writing for a few years now."

"Never thought of you as the sensitive type. Not Mr. Athlete of the Year."

"Growing up, sports, music, and you were all I thought about. I started keeping a journal while in Afghanistan, then ventured into other writing when I came back to the States."

And did he still think about her, about the way they once were? "What do you write?"

"Articles, stories about life here in Brookside. I write songs too."

"Are you published?"

He shook his head, his expression bashful. "No. I only write for pleasure."

This man who occupied the adult body of the Dwight Etting she once knew suddenly seemed a stranger, yet someone she'd like to know better. The pain that followed prom really wasn't his fault—and the blame was hers. Dwight never knew, and she never planned on telling him. If only she could find the strength to let go of her resentment and take responsibility for her choices.

Perhaps life purified that pubescent Dwight. Did he think she had changed as well? If so, his opinion of her must be lower than ever, given the way he acted toward her, polite yet distanced. Not that she blamed him for ill thoughts. There were days she didn't like the woman she'd become either. What could she do about it? Her course had been set, with a wedding only a few weeks away.

Fiddlers Fling

They finished shopping and headed back to Daddy's house ... the place she used to call home. She pushed the remorse aside and Dwight unload supplies. Monday, she'd call Nursing Services to explore options for long-term care. If her father refused, she'd swallow her pride enough to ask Robert for legal advice.

Dwight put the plastic bags into the recycling container. "I'll check on you tomorrow. I have to go to the office for a few minutes before church. You said you hadn't been in a while, but I wondered if you'd like to go tomorrow ... with me ... to pray for your father."

"Don't need to go to church for that. As I recall, God hears our prayers wherever we are."

"Still true."

Should she tell him she'd already planned on going? She had to find some way of renewing a friendship with him, if for no other reason than to help Daddy. She had despised Dwight for too long. Church might help her find peace—peace that eluded her all these years. "Okay, but I'll drive myself."

Dwight frowned. "If that's what you want." He turned to leave, then pivoted to face her. "There's one question I need to ask."

"I won't promise an answer."

"Fair enough. Are you aware you have your father's power of attorney? After you left home, both our fathers amended the partnership agreement in the event of either's incapacitation so that their children—you and me—could step in on their behalf."

She plopped down on a stool.

Dwight raised his eyebrows. "I'll take that as a no. Dad wrote me about the decision. Apparently Big Mike never told you."

"That's a lot to take in at this moment. If my father won't cooperate, in order to manage his affairs, would I have to prove him incompetent? I agree with Louise. I think he's more stubborn than incapacitated."

"Sounds like a legal question. Know a good lawyer?"

Dwight sat in his truck, praying before he returned to his apartment. Way to ruin a great restart with Jolene. He'd been abrupt as always, tact never his strong suit, his smart-aleck remarks an adolescent trademark and one he needed to grow out of.

40

With typical Jolene Murdock fierceness, she'd pushed him out the door. He'd let her cool down until morning. Maybe she'd be willing to look over the company records after church ... if she still came. From his earliest memories, Jolene Murdock wore defiance like a badge of honor. Her stubbornness, though frustrating, made her impossibly more beautiful. All five-feet-two-inches of her modeled a spitfire-independence that challenged him, yet was the very stuff that drew him to her. If only he could forget she belonged to another man.

Chapter Six

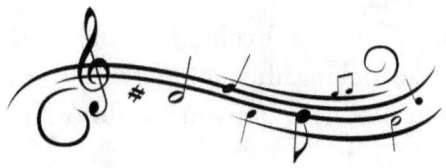

Jolene put away the supply of cereal, meat, potatoes, vegetables, and cleaning products. If nothing else, the refrigerator would be stocked with healthy foods and the house spic-and-span. Take a little burden off the kindly neighbor.

She'd have bought fruit, but Daddy never ate anything that wasn't cooked to beef jerky consistency. Amazing that he ate Louise's casseroles. Jolene rummaged through the cupboards, filled more with beer bottles than real food. She should confront Daddy, tell him his drinking only made the cancer worse, that his drinking was over, or ...

Or what? What recourse did she have? How much authority did her power of attorney give her? Did it include medical decisions? At least he had the common sense not to drive. She'd have hated to make him turn over his car keys. Dwight said the power of attorney was durable. She'd need to see a copy. Where had it been filed? Had it been registered? As a social worker, her knowledge of power of attorney options was quite extensive. Her father would be unable to change the power of attorney if she proved mental incapacitation. Even so, he'd fight her—resistance the core of his personality. No legal document would hold back Big Mike Murdock's indomitable will.

The knock on the door startled her, and she dropped the dishcloth on the floor. She picked it up and threw it in the trash. Filthy anyway, like washing a counter with·mud. Tomorrow, she'd buy an assortment of kitchen linens.

Fiddlers Fling

When she opened the door, Louise stood there holding a baking pan wrapped in aluminum foil. "I worried you hadn't had anything to eat, so I whipped up this lasagna. Dwight makes sure your father eats on the weekends, but the only thing he can cook is hamburgers."

Jolene's stomach roiled at so much food. If Dwight and Louise kept feeding her, she'd gain so much weight she wouldn't fit into her wedding dress. "Thank you, but I did have supper at Dwight's house." She snickered. "Hamburgers, of course. We shopped and stocked the house with canned goods and cleaning supplies."

Louise scowled. "Well, dear, I could have done that for you if I had a list to work with. I like looking after your father."

"I appreciate your kindness, but you shouldn't have to go to so much personal expense."

Daddy came downstairs. "Is that you, Louise? What did you bring?"

Louise smiled, like a flower opening with the morning sun. "Lasagna, Michael. The way you like it. Extra cheese, and cooked so's it's crispy, not runny, and with plenty of sausage."

He passed by Jolene, no acknowledgement of her presence, and hauled out a stack of paper plates. "Will you join me, Louise?"

Jolene gasped at the change in him. The father she remembered had a round belly, glossy white hair and a full beard, neatly cropped. This man's eyes, a muted blue, lacked Daddy's twinkle. His former sunbathed skin was now yellowed. How progressed was his disease? Couldn't something be done for him? How does one ask the question, "How soon before you die?"

Jolene's stomach ached from feeling overfull, Dwight's hamburger rivaling two Big Macs in size. Her father might not talk to her, but he apparently responded to Louise's cooking. "On second thought, Louise, that lasagna looks inviting. I think I will join you. Daddy, would you mind getting me a plate, too?"

"Already did. Another one for Dwight in case he stops by."

Louise took the plates and set the table, the lasagna taking a position of honor in the middle. "I'll boil water for instant coffee, Michael. It should be ready by the time you get out of the shower."

He nodded and went upstairs.

"Jolene, you didn't happen to buy any dish detergent while you were shopping, did you?"

"Underneath the sink."

Louise opened the cupboard door and examined Jolene's purchase. "Not the kind I like to use, but it'll do. Did you buy any coffee? He was just about out of what I brought last week."

"Yes. Colombian."

Jolene found the can and handed it to Louise.

"Good brand. Michael likes his coffee so strong a cinnamon stick could stand up straight in it. Trouble is, his pot ain't working, so I have to make instant."

Jolene pointed to the counter. "I bought a new coffee maker, an auto-drip."

"We'll see. If Michael notices it, he'll dump the coffee out. He'll only drink brewed coffee if it's made in a percolator. His ain't safe ... has a short in it."

"I should have remembered that was the only coffee he drank."

"If you wanna keep that automatic for yourself, I suggest you hide it somewhere Michael won't see it. Lord only knows where that might be. I swear, he's got the nose of a bloodhound. Purposely goes looking to see if anything's different."

Daddy came back down, his hair slicked back and smelling of Old Spice.

Louise asked, "Any fruit, Jolene?"

"No, I didn't buy any. Daddy, you never eat fruit, right? I remember you liked your vegetables cooked to near charcoal and your beef like Texas Tack."

Louise smiled. "That so, Michael? You always eat whatever I bring over. Jolene, check in the pantry. There's some canned."

Daddy rubbed his stomach. "Store-bought just doesn't have the same flavor."

Jolene found the mason jars filled with peaches and brought them to Louise. She divided the contents three ways, making sure Daddy had extra. She prepared the instant coffee, then set it on the table.

Daddy turned toward the pantry. "There's plasticware in there."

Jolene frowned. Years past, Daddy frowned on paper products, claiming the environment could use a rest.

"I know I should get back to using real plates and things, but I hate washing dishes." He glanced toward the counter. "What's that auto-drip doing there?"

Jolene shook her head. So much she'd forgotten, and so many things had changed. She felt a stranger in the only home she'd known before she left. "I bought it. I'll exchange it for a percolator tomorrow."

"Percolator would be nice. But I don't want you spending your own money. Hope you didn't buy anything else. Make a list of what I owe you. I'll go to the bank tomorrow."

"Doc Benson doesn't want you driving no more, Michael," Louise interjected. "And tomorrow's Sunday."

"I can write a check for cash at the store. Don't care what Doc says. I'll drive if I want to."

Louise shrugged. "Suit yourself."

He ambled to the table and sat down next to Louise. Jolene sat at the end of the table on Louise's other side. Daddy gobbled his food, hardly taking time to swallow. "Good as always." Picking up his plate and plasticware, he dumped them into the trash, then wandered into the den, turning the television on to the *History Channel*.

Louise cleaned off the table. "You hardly touched yours, Jolene."

"The lasagna was delicious. As I told you, I had plenty to eat at Dwight's."

Louise joined Daddy in the den, leaving Jolene alone in the kitchen.

Dwight had said her father wasn't managing well. By the looks of things, with the help of good people like Louise, he could stay at home for a long time. About all Jolene needed to do was to set up an account for Louise so she didn't have to dip into her own funds. Or was Daddy giving her money? Was that the source of her good will?

Jolene took out the notepad she'd bought earlier and went through the cupboards, making a list of other needed items. She went to the laundry room. The old Westinghouse washer and dryer were still there and looked to be the same set as from her earliest memory. Not surprising he'd never replaced them, since his mantra was, "Why get new when a few replaced nuts and bolts will get it up and running again?"

If only new hardware could fix Daddy.

Jolene startled at a noise and turned to see Louise coming in from the kitchen, carrying an armful of dirty clothes. "Michael went upstairs to go to bed and threw down his laundry for me to wash."

"I could probably do that, Louise."

"Your father's washer and dryer ain't working. No telling how long they been broke. You'd have to go to the laundromat clear on the other side of town. I don't mind doing things for him. Truth is, I'm hard-put to fill up my days what with my man gone on to glory. So you'd be doing me a favor if you let me help out a bit."

"I appreciate everything you've done. How long have you been coming over?"

"For a month or two, after I heard how bad things were. At first he didn't let me in the door. Now he lets me do a few things for him. Mostly he just wants me to sit and eat with him. He's a talker, that one."

"Daddy? He never said more than a sentence at a time while I was growing up."

"That's the way of men, dear. They get so talked out at work or their meetings, home's just a place to unwind and be quiet. I suppose he likes to talk to me and Dwight 'cause we're about the only folks he sees. When I take him out in the car on occasion, he likes to stop in and see a few of his old friends, and grunt and groan about politics."

"I've started a shopping list. I'll go to the store tomorrow."

"Best be careful before you go replacing things. Michael don't miss a thing. Dwight and me have both tried."

"We'll let tomorrow take care of tomorrow."

"Sounds like something Michael would say."

Jolene smiled with the memory. "His exact words were, 'Don't worry about tomorrow today. Let tomorrow take care of tomorrow.' He said it came from the Bible."

Louise laughed—a soft giggle, like that of a young girl's, as she stuffed Daddy's dirty clothes into a bag. "Michael sure does like to rewrite Scripture." She rewrapped the lasagna with aluminum foil, then put the container in the refrigerator. "Enough left for your supper tomorrow."

"Thank you. I know how to cook. I can manage for a few days."

Louise harrumphed as she picked up the bag of laundry. "I hope you're not going to stick Michael away in some old nursing home. Though I suppose it's none of my business."

Absolutely right, Louise.

Jolene breathed a sigh of relief when Louise closed the door. Something in her manner seemed incongruent with normal kindliness, as if motivated more by a need to be needed.

Fiddlers Fling

Jolene gathered the trash, then went to the back porch where the garbage bags used to be stored. She found an old galvanized steel can overflowing with poorly sealed bags. Was no one picking up the trash? She wrote that on her list of things she needed to check. Who paid his household bills? She'd have to inquire with the utility companies, notify the bank, and arrange to have her father's bills sent to her. If the company was nearing bankruptcy, was Daddy broke too?

Questions flooded in so fast her head hurt.

Let tomorrow take care of tomorrow.

A strong need for sleep took precedence for immediate answers to a parade of questions. First, she'd investigate the upstairs and peek into her old room ... maybe take a few things back to Albany with her. Snorts and snores indicated Daddy was probably out for the night. She'd hoped to talk with him but was grateful she hadn't been completely ignored.

She opened the door to her room and hit the light switch, gasping at the sight. Holes spotted the walls. The room appeared to be stripped of everything, her past reduced to a vacant spot where once she read, played her music, danced to her fantasies, and talked to Dwight on the phone for hours. Her eyes misted, and she shook her head. No tears. Foolish to think reconciliation might be possible. She should never have come home. She'd do what little she could for her father, then return to Albany as soon as possible. Let Louise take over since that's what she wanted.

Jolene closed the bedroom door. She'd have to stay at the Ashworth estate after all.

She drove the four miles to the mammoth house where exterior floodlights cast a specter on the estate, a perfect backdrop for a Norman Bates sequel.

She'd always thought the house grotesque, though tourists claimed it exuded old-world charm. The main portion of the house was built in 1808 by the first Ashworth to come to Brookside. Since that time, an Ashworth had occupied the domicile, though many ancestors owned additional homes elsewhere. Robert's grandparents lived in the Catskills, and an uncle lived in the Berkshires. Some extended family had migrated to Florida and southern Georgia. Robert's parents spent weeks at a time visiting this villa or that. Mother Mary insisted Jolene travel with them when Robert's meetings kept him away.

She pulled into the circular drive. A middle-aged man, dressed in a vest and leather cap, came out to meet her. "I'm David. I take care of the yards and the vehicles. Mrs. Ashworth notified me you'd be staying here and instructed me to assist you with anything you need. The maid left an hour ago, but your room is ready. What time do you want your car for the morning?"

"Would eight be okay?"

"Eight it is. It'll be gassed up and ready to go. There's a security guard who checks on the premises at night. Otherwise, the house will be empty."

Jolene laughed. "This is Brookside. Nothing much happens here."

"Just the same, a lady alone can't be too careful. Would you prefer I stay over?"

"No need."

David handed her a card with a list of phone numbers. "That's the guard's phone. Mine's on there too in case you need anything. Be sure to program them into your cell. Wouldn't want you to forget where you put the numbers in the event they're needed—though there are panic buttons throughout the house."

She nodded. "Thanks. I'll do that."

David took out her suitcase. "Where would you like me to put this?"

"Here, give it to me and go on home. You probably stayed late waiting for me to get here."

David tipped his hat. "Thank you, ma'am. See you in the morning."

With that, he drove Jolene's BMW out of sight to some unknown place where the Ashworths parked their vehicles. She should have asked for a map.

She once read an article about the Brookside Ashworths and how their family heritage resembled the Oyster Bay Roosevelts—American aristocracy. Daddy's lineage was more in keeping with pioneers. Mother Mary drummed the sentiment day in and day out. "Destiny is what you make, dear, not what happens to you."

She found her room and marveled at the white upholstered three-quarter bed, clothed with a down duvet. The lace curtains blew with a late spring breeze coming through the open window. She set her purse on the Louis XVI side chair while she unpacked her suitcase. Putting her newly bought jeans and tees into the nine-drawer cedar dresser, she laughed at the juxtaposition— her twenty-dollar jeans housed in a dresser that probably cost two grand. Next, she tucked her jewelry into the walnut armoire. She lined the marble counter with an assortment of beauty products, the arsenal Mother Mary had insisted a well-groomed politician's wife needed. Jolene had resisted at first. Ironic that now she knew every brand.

She opened the white embossed writing table to store her notebook, then sent a text to Robert to let him know she'd settled in. She brought up Dwight's number. Although still upset over his lawyer comment, didn't courtesy dictate he know where she'd be staying for the next few days? Besides, even though she was promised to another man, right or wrong, she liked the sound of his voice. He could have been a broadcaster, his inflection precise and with a pleasant baritone.

He answered on the first ring. "Jolene? Everything okay?"

"You didn't tell me the upstairs was worse than the downstairs."

"You mean Big Mike's house?"

"I hoped maybe I could stay in my old room. I hate this mansion."

"You could stay with me."

"I don't think so. Funny. I've never been inside this Ashworth estate before."

"Is it as creepy inside as out?"

"From the little I've seen, yes. Maybe I could hire someone to help clean my father's house. Know somebody?"

"You could always hire Louise. You should have seen the place before she started coming over."

Worse than it is now? "I suppose, but I'm afraid she wouldn't accept money, and she's already going out of her way with kindness."

"Ever think maybe there's more than kindness at work?"

"What does that mean? Is Louise a thief?"

"No. I mean your father's capable of doing a lot more for himself than he does. I think he likes Louise's company."

"I don't think he cares for mine."

"Give him time."

How much time will it take? "Goodnight. I'll see you tomorrow."

She disconnected, feeling as though she'd just made a date.

She glanced at the painted dual mirrors, similar to those Mother Mary had furnished for the guest house. Why so much of one design in any place an Ashworth inhabited? As much as she despised the period, Jolene was jarred with the realization she could name every stick of furniture, where it could be bought, and how much it cost. Daddy's idea of décor consisted of a couch, recliner, dressers, and end tables all bought at a thrift store, her grandmother's quilts the only antique items in the house besides broken appliances.

She peered into the mirrors, her clothes ruined. She tossed them into the trash. Pity. The money spent on her outfit could have fed a homeless man for months. Truth be known, though, she didn't regret the afternoon romp, the freedom to abandon herself to frivolity, moments so rare since she left Brookside. Why? Had she become a younger version of Mother Mary, always attuned to propriety ... the kind of woman Dwight used to ridicule?

She twirled, taking a harder examination of herself from head to toe. Who was this persona staring back at her? She unclamped the Jane Tran hairclip and smoothed her long, straight blonde tresses over her shoulders. She went into the bath and turned on the shower, nauseated at the cluttered cosmetic assortment on the counter. She threw them back into her suitcase, naming each expensive brand like a curse word. Since she'd be in Brookside only a few days, she didn't need anything more than a little face moisturizer and mascara. What better opportunity to throw convention to the wind before she'd have to walk the aisle toward absolute respectability?

Chapter Seven

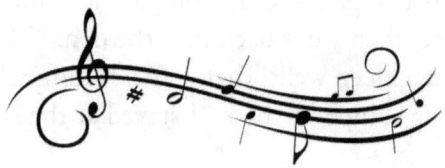

The room filled with eerie gray, no hint of morning coming through the window. She turned in bed and faced the clock. Still earlier than a rooster's wake-up call. Might as well get up. She should have known better than to drink coffee so late. She called David, sorry to have awakened him, and asked him to get the car ready earlier than expected. The sweet man didn't even grumble. Whatever the Ashworths paid him wasn't enough.

She dressed in a long black knitted skirt and red top, a go-anywhere-not-too-flashy-for-church outfit. Reaching for the Jane Tran, she pulled her hair up. *No!* She giggled in her defiance as she threw the hair clip into the trash on top of yesterday's discarded clothes. She shook her head and let her hair fall unencumbered, grabbed her newly purchased faux-leather purse, and headed toward the car. The BMW was warming up, David waiting patiently nearby until she drove off, a narrow crack of red in the dark sky.

She should check on her father before church.

Daddy used to rise hours before the sun. Would he be up? No lights inside. She parked, shuddering at the exterior bleakness, more disturbing in the pre-dawn hours. When she entered the house, *Family Feud* reruns blared from the den. Was the show on twenty-four hours a day?

She peeked in. He sat in front of the television, probably unaware she stood behind him. Should she try to talk to him?

Why risk rejection?

She went into the kitchen and boiled water for his coffee, putting two scoops of instant into a Styrofoam cup, the way Louise had made it yesterday, the aroma welcoming. Jolene scrambled four eggs, putting two slices of bread into the toaster before she discovered the broken electric coils. Fearing he might get a shock or worse, she threw the toaster out and started a list of items she needed to buy besides a toaster and percolator. She added dinnerware to the list. Daddy probably wouldn't use it for himself, but Louise might prefer to eat off real dishes since she shared so many meals with him. The three plates Jolene had found were mismatched and badly chipped.

She filled two paper plates and brought them into the dining room along with the coffee, then went back into the den. "Morning, Daddy."

"Morning, Jolene. Sleep well? That couch is lumpy."

A cordial greeting. Hope birthed. "I stayed at the Ashworth estate last night."

"I didn't make you. Though I'm not surprised you think your old home not good enough for you."

She let the comment slide. "I made breakfast. Will you have it with me?"

"I could eat."

He sat down at the table, and in the morning light, without Louise bustling around, Jolene studied the man, still stunned at the changes—his sallow cheeks and slow gait.

He devoured his eggs in his usual three bites, nibbled his toast, then tossed the plate into the garbage, retreating to the den. What had she expected? Daddy used to eat breakfast by himself and left the house before she got up for school. Did she expect him to suddenly change his ways because she was home?

She glanced out the window, the sun peeking over the horizon. Still early. What else could she do? She'd make biscuits. She enjoyed the challenge of baking without proper tools. She found an unused paint stick, washed it off, and used that in place of a wooden spoon. Wax paper? She searched the pantry. *God bless Louise!*

No rolling pin or biscuit-cutter. Jolene clicked her tongue with inspiration. Rolling out the dough with a paper cup, she used a second one and cut the dough around its bottom to shape the biscuits. She put her creation into the oven and inhaled the scent of freshly baked bread, anticipating how they'd taste with the butter she bought.

Funny how, as a teenager, she resented helping out at home. She'd resisted ironing, cleaning, sewing, and washing dishes. Yet when she donned an apron, she was an artist, a creator of sorts, baking—her second love next to music. Pity that neither pastime fit her new lifestyle.

What need did she have to cook? She dined with the Ashworths, either at their home or in fancy restaurants. While the chefs prepared tasty meals, she missed the rewards of preparing one's own food. Did Mother Mary even know how to boil water?

Jolene put two biscuits aside for lunch and stored the rest in the freezer. She walked back into the den and tapped her father on the shoulder. "I'm going to church. I'm not sure when I'll be back. I put out two biscuits and a can of soup for lunch. Promise me you'll eat something?"

He stared at his grimy fingernails.

"Daddy? Did you hear me?"

"Yeah. You do whatever you want. I ain't going nowhere."

"And you'll eat lunch as I asked?"

"If I'm hungry."

Or maybe Louise would happen by.

She remembered seeing a discount store outside of town on her way into Brookside, about a mile from Community Church. She glanced at her watch. She had enough time to buy a percolator, toaster, and some dinnerware. She'd keep the receipts, let her father pay if he insisted.

The Ashworths employed personal shoppers and only purchased from places like Nordstroms, almost always at exaggerated prices. Brookside's idea of a high-end mercantile was the Sears store in the next town over.

Not many shoppers on a Sunday morning apparently. Jolene grabbed a cart and looked for the small appliance aisle. She hadn't noticed Alicia Davenport until she stood in front of Jolene's cart. Odd that Alicia would be at a discount store, her shopping habits were as snooty as the Ashworths.

"Hello, Jolene."

"Alicia? Slumming, I see."

She laughed, as phony an offering as her pasty smile that heightened her devilishly silk black hair. "I was about to say the same thing to you—about this store, I mean. I knew you were in Brookside. Robert called. He asked me to keep an eye out in case you needed anything."

"You followed me?"

Fiddlers Fling

She laughed again, a high-pitched *do-ti-la-sol* downward-scale-guffaw like a horse's neigh. "I haven't been stalking you if that's what you're implying. I needed milk. This store is close by. Milk is milk. I was about to check out when I saw you enter." Alicia hitched her $1500 purse over her shoulder, a brand Jolene recognized as even more expensive than her Michael Kors heels she'd put in the closet when she switched to more sensible shoes for Brookside. Suddenly, the complete lunacy of carrying a top-of-the-line handbag to a discount store brought an involuntary snicker, disguised as a cough.

In high school, she'd used a paisley tote; in college, a book-bag, and had been content with any arrangement to carry belongings from one place to another. Last week, she'd asked Robert's New York City shopper to pick her up a pair of Mother Mary-approved Valentino shoes. Bit by bit, she'd become seduced by upper-class snobbery.

Like a spaghetti western, the two women glared at one another, curling their bottom lips, waiting for the other to draw an oral weapon, until Alicia broke the stalemate. "And what brings you here on a Sunday morning?"

None of your business, sweetie. "Running an errand for my father."

"How is he?"

"As good as can be expected, given his circumstances."

Alicia tilted her head. "That bad?"

"Weakened, of course, but he's able to get around, and his mental capacity seems basically intact. I think his forgetfulness is purposeful. What worries me is his attitude, as if he simply doesn't care. Like he's given up." Jolene glanced at her watch. "I should get going. I thought I'd go to church today."

"I didn't think you were the religious type."

"I grew up in a home of faith. My father insisted I attend church twice on Sundays and every prayer meeting. Robert and I go on occasion."

"He's wise to do so. Christians are voters." Alicia could put a political spin on generic toothpaste.

"I thought I'd visit the church where I grew up."

"I heard Big Mike gave up going to church when you left home."

Not a stretch that Alicia knew about Jolene's argument with her father, attuned as she was to town gossip, and Robert told his campaign manager everything. Still, personal family business should not be fodder for political gain.

Alicia leaned provocatively against her cart. "Are those bags under your eyes? Did you forget to bring your makeup?"

"Didn't sleep well last night. A little overwhelmed."

"With?"

"My father's situation, changes in Brookside."

"What did you expect to find?"

"Hope."

"You have a fantastic future ahead of you. As for your father, don't worry. I've already developed a press release that my candidate's fiancée has come home on an errand of mercy for her terminally ill father. The story is sure to garner sympathy and more votes."

Jolene forced a smile to hide her anger. "I should only be in Brookside a few more days and will be back on the campaign trail with New York's next state senator."

"Good. Robert needs you by his side. The fewer questions asked the better. Call me if you need anything." With that Alicia sashayed toward the exit ... without milk. Of course she'd been spying.

Jolene texted Robert. *Don't appreciate your putting Alicia on my tail. I want it stopped.*

Within seconds, her cell rang. "Yes, Robert."

"You actually answered."

"I thought I'd re-emphasize my text. I can't stand that woman. Why did you pick her for a campaign manager? I think she annoys everyone in Brookside."

"No one else knows our family better."

True enough, according to Mother Mary. Alicia Davenport was the daughter of a prominent family friend.

"You're not jealous, are you?"

She spotted an antique-looking toaster that resembled Daddy's. "Of course not. Should I be?"

She clicked the cell to speaker, set her purse in the top section of her cart, then slipped the phone next to the purse, turning her attention on the boxed percolator from the top shelf, shimmying it to a spot where she could grab it.

"No need to be jealous. We weren't engaged that long."

Jolene dropped the box with enough force to move the cart ahead three feet. She trotted after it and snatched the phone from the cart. "You and

Alicia were engaged? When were you going to tell me that little piece of information? On our honeymoon?"

Robert laughed. "I broke it off when you came to work for us. You're the only woman for me, Jolene."

"You have a funny way of declaring your love, but I'll take that last statement in the spirit I hope it was meant. Just make sure I don't run into Alicia Davenport again."

"Brookside's a small town. How much longer before you return to Albany? People are asking where you are." He whispered, "I miss you."

"I should hope so. I'm late for church. I'll call you later." She disconnected before Robert could convince her not to attend.

Dwight glanced around the sanctuary, then checked the sound quality on his keyboard while Jack tuned his guitar. The vibrate mode on his cell signaled a message from Jolene—*running late.* He tapped a hurried reply— *in worship band/see you after service.* He took his place on the platform, eyes glued toward the entryway, his heart skipping a beat when she finally walked in. She sat regally, crossing her legs at the ankles, unlike the tomboy he'd grown up with. Something had happened to that girl. He sensed the imprisoned spirit that once drove sixteen-year-old Jolene Murdock to adventure now cried to be loosed. Was it his place to help her rediscover the better part of her? Or should he take a backseat and let her plow full-speed toward her destruction?

The worship team began their praise set with "Here I Am to Worship," the words settling deep in his heart. As a youth, his church music had been more about performance. Since coming home from Afghanistan, familiar choruses became a personal expression of the new and improved Dwight Etting, thanks to saving grace. Next the band played "Great and Mighty." Within seconds, Jack's scowl signified his displeasure at Dwight's speed. Yet how can one slow down a song that testifies to God's power? The congregation showed their agreement with heartfelt clapping.

Dwight kept one eye on Jolene during the worship songs. She remained subdued, more an observer than a participant. Growing up, she sang with the youth praise team, sometimes adding her fiddle to instrumentals. How much of her music had her fiancé forced her to give up?

Dwight smiled throughout Pastor Tim's homily, wondering how a man could speak for thirty minutes without notes.—a gift Dwight lacked. He'd always been slow in speech, but not with Jolene. Words weren't necessary—their time together had been filled with sledding, riding, or playing with Goldie in the fields behind his farm. He remembered that night by the fireplace in the cabin when words weren't necessary. But things were never the same between them after that. Guilt? Between camp meetings and Sunday school lessons, he'd been warned against sex outside of marriage. He'd failed Jolene. He should have been stronger, protected her.

Instead of confessing how he felt, he found excuses not to be alone with her. Now she hated him. If only he had Ashworth's silver tongue. Right or wrong, the man knew how to win over a crowd, rendering as convincing an argument as Pastor Tim. Was that what attracted Jolene to Ashworth? If so, Dwight could never compete.

Chapter Eight

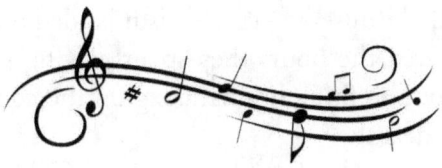

Jolene folded and slipped the church bulletin into her purse. Might be a good idea to request a visit from Pastor Tim. Being new, he might not be aware of her father's circumstances.

Dwight approached, and Jolene swallowed hard. His black slacks and yellow Oxford shirt set off his sandy-colored hair and chocolate eyes, a hammer-wielding local who could double for a male fashion model.

Her face warmed to sense Dwight's appeal, wrong that she should be attracted to any man other than her fiancé. Although the latest article she'd read in *Contemplating Marriage* said couples should, in fact, notice and appreciate the other sex ... as long as they didn't take the fantasy outside the relationship. Seemed contradictory to what her Sunday school teachers preached, the thought being as bad as the deed.

Was Dwight temptation? He was once ... more than she could handle.

She'd paid for her sin. When she and Robert started dating soon after she'd moved to Albany, she'd led him to believe in her innocence, insisting they stay pure for their marriage bed. Would he guess she wasn't a virgin?

She gulped again when Dwight stood next to her, his cologne reminiscent of the fields behind his house. His smile added to his allure. "Glad you came, Jolene."

"You look good." The words spewed in spite of an inner siren.

"Thanks. You do too."

He shrugged—a boyish blush in his cheeks, his smile evoking old desires.

Fiddlers Fling

Dwight put on his baseball cap, an odd addition to his otherwise prep-school image. "Ready to go?"

She shouldn't be alone with him, but she needed to see the accounts. "I'll follow you over."

The office was much as she remembered—a large, single room with couch, television, desk, shelves, and file cabinets. Dwight tossed his cap toward the coat rack. "Bullseye," he said, as it landed on an empty peg.

Jolene remembered the hours they spent playing ring-toss and darts. Sometimes she won. She flung her handbag on the couch. "A little heavy to toss. You win by default."

"Didn't know we were having a contest. But I still have my dartboard." He went to a cedar closet and flung open the door. "Want to make it interesting?"

"Yeah? How so?"

"Whoever loses has to cook lunch."

Jolene picked up a dart, positioned herself at an imaginary line, and threw, landing on the innermost ring. They took turns until Dwight conceded. "I have leftover pizza in the fridge if you're hungry."

"Sure."

He closed the closet door, took out the pizza, and put it in the microwave.

"Soda, coffee, or water?"

"Diet Coke?"

"No diet soda here, lady."

"Water's fine."

He handed her the pizza and a bottle of water. "I suppose you'd like a napkin."

"Unless you want to look at a sauce-face."

He went to a cupboard and came back with a fistful of napkins, popped open his soda, and took a sip. Combining aromas of pepperoni and melted mozzarella stoked her appetite. She took a large bite. "This actually tastes good. Can't remember the last time I had pizza."

"Why's that?"

"Most of Robert's campaign contributors don't hang out at pizza parlors. Once in a while, I'll fake a headache and go out for fast food."

"My, but you are the rebel, aren't you?"

She met Dwight's eyes and felt a hunger for something other than pizza. She put her slice down. "I suppose I should look at the accounts."

"I don't have a lot of financial info here. We have someone who manages receivables and payables."

"Then how's my father's illness causing problems for the company?"

"Big Mike legally has to sign off on the paperwork. He refuses, except to pay the men. No money coming in means no money's going out. Can't pay our bills and can't pay the workers. As his power of attorney, you can sign for him or arrange to give me authority. As it stands now, we'll be bankrupt within a couple of months."

"When did things start going bad?"

"Not long after you left. At first, he only drank a couple of beers a day. Now it's a six-pack. He pretty much lost interest. Didn't show up at the worksites and wouldn't sign paperwork or pay the bills. I should have told you about his drinking when I called."

How much more had Dwight kept from her? "Why didn't you?"

"Thought it might change your mind about coming, and you'd find out soon enough after you got here."

Had Dwight used her sympathy to gain control of Daddy's company? "Be easier all around if you signed the contracts."

She paced.

"You're still hesitant?"

"I don't want to take away my father's independence, and I don't think it's come to that just yet. His incompetence, his excessive drinking—I think those are just symptoms, not caused by an inability to cope with his diagnosis. I think there's something else behind his apathy."

"Spoken like a true left-wing bleeding heart. Look, I care about your father too. I don't want to see him lose his independence any more than you do. But something has got to change. And I'm looking to you to decide what. I never studied psychology. I don't want to tell you what to do, but sometimes the loving thing is the most difficult."

Dwight went to the filing cabinet and held up a large folder. "The thing is, we need to act soon. Six months ago, we had over one-hundred men on our payroll. We're down to forty, and there's not enough capital to pay the workers I have left. In here are four new contracts that would allow me to hire back most of the crew and keep the business afloat another year. So far Big Mike has refused to sign them."

"Bring the contracts over this evening. I'll see what I can do. If I can't get him to sign, I'll do it and deal with the repercussions later."

Jolene rose and walked to the window. The afternoon had sped by, and dark clouds hid the sun. "I've never known my father to give up. He's a fighter, like all the Murdocks before him. It's not the cancer. What devoured his spirit?"

Dwight bit his lower lip.

"Say what you're thinking."

"It's you, Jolene. You're the root cause. He gave up hope you'd ever come back to Brookside."

Jolene drove to her father's house. Television sounds reverberated from the den. While growing up, the house shook with music, not *Ancient Aliens* re-runs. Funny how Daddy fixated on game shows, documentaries, and the news, switching channels like a kid runs from toy to toy, aimless, without purpose.

She went to the den. "Daddy, Dwight's coming over for dinner."

"I like that boy. Wish you were marrying him instead of young Ashworth."

"There's no chance that'll happen."

Prom night had ended any future with Dwight Etting. Eleanor Roosevelt counseled young women to make their futures wherever Providence put them. Jolene's future belonged with Robert Ashworth.

"Daddy, we need to talk."

"Nothing to say." As if to emphasize the point, he turned up the volume.

"Dwight's bringing papers over for you to sign."

"Won't sign nothin'. You can if you want to. I gave you the right."

"Don't you care what happens to your business?"

"Nope. Everything goes to you when I die. So if you marry Ashworth, he'll get it all. If I let the company go to Hades, won't be anything left for him to take."

His logic made sense in a twisted way. Jolene turned off the television. She expected ire. Instead, he silently met her gaze. "If I act as your power of attorney, I'm doing as I think you want things done, not what Robert says. I can fix it so he gets nothing."

"You might think that. Might even try. But the Ashworths have you right where they want you."

"Don't you care about the men you have working for you? Don't you remember why you and Ken started the company in the first place? Dwight says he's had to lay off over half the workforce. What chance do you think they'll have of finding other work in Brookside? Besides, Murdock & Etting has always been an important factor in Brookside economics. Your company's failure will hurt the town."

"I knew sending you off to college was a mistake. You're so smart, what do you suggest?"

"Sign the contracts, Daddy."

"Won't do it."

He snatched the remote and turned the television back on.

Dwight hesitated at the door a few seconds to utter a prayer, not sure what to expect other than hoping Jolene would show a little appreciation for his efforts. After all, he'd inconvenienced himself to help Big Mike. Though if Jolene had asked him to walk on water, he'd have found a way to comply.

When he entered the kitchen, she shot him a helpless glance.

"No-go, I take it," he said.

"Daddy refuses to get involved. Good news is he doesn't care if I step in or not."

Dwight spread out the contracts on the counter. Nothing to keep her from signing now. "Then—"

"Not just yet. Give me a few days. I still think it's important that Daddy sign them." She glanced toward the garbage bin. "Funny. I haven't noticed any beer bottles in the trash since I took the bag out."

"See, your being here is having a positive impact already."

If she was the cause of her father's retreat to alcohol abuse, would he pick the bottle back up when she left again? Would a few days really make that much difference? When Big Mike Murdock made a decision, no argument short of an angelic visit convinced him otherwise. Dwight tucked the contracts back into the folder. "I won't badger you, but the longer we delay, the more men I may have to let go."

Dwight glanced into the den. "Still can't get over seeing your father like this, watching television all day long. I remember how active he used to be. Never saw him sitting, even when he played the fiddle."

Jolene leaned forward, her hair falling over her shoulders. "Let me look at the contracts."

"Here."

She curled a few wanton strands around her fingers as she read them. He sat next to her, her perfume inviting. Hard to be so close, her scent like strong drink. He resisted the urge to sweep her into his arms.

She's not yours, Dwight.

She stretched and went to the kitchen, returning with percolated coffee and two slices of apple pie."

"Louise's?"

"Mine."

Dwight took a hearty bite. *Delicious!* "Way better than Louise's."

Jolene smirked as she returned to business, scouring over the contracts. He paced, interjecting his opinions here and there.

Sometimes she scowled, and at other times, she licked her lips,—beautiful lips he wanted to kiss, lightly colored with strawberry lipstick. At times, she raised her head and peered as if deep in her thoughts. Was he in them?

Dwight handed her another folder.

"These are the bankruptcy papers I've kept on hand, hoping I wouldn't have to have Big Mike file them."

Jolene glanced back at the documents. "Dwight, what's going on here? I don't think the company's financial problems are all related to poor management."

She'd come home looking like a runway model, and he'd forgotten she'd made honor roll all four years of high school and dean's list in college. She saw through the cleverest camouflage. He shouldn't have kept the truth from her.

"I can't tell you without breaking my promise."

"What promise?"

"To not bad-mouth Robert or his family."

"Tell me."

"It's complicated."

She stood, her face crimson. "Why does every man think every blonde is dumb? I had a minor in economics, and don't forget I worked for Daddy during summer vacations."

"Let's take a walk, and I'll try to explain."

Fresh air produced fresh thoughts. He breathed in and out, cleansing his lungs as they strolled in silence toward the riverbank, one of their favorite places to sit and talk ... or make out. Early June in the North Country brought anything from blistering hot days or cold rain flecked with snowflakes, sometimes weather extremes within the same day. Today, balmy temperatures dominated. The clouds still bunched together, but the threat of fresh rain had passed. Moisture, left from yesterday's heavy rains, clung to peeping greenery while the sun beamed on dandelions populating grassy knolls.

Her pace lagged behind. He stopped when they reached the open field at the water's edge and let her catch up.

She glared. "Okay, I want the unvarnished truth. Rip it, Etting."

He took a deep breath and jumped in. "For the last six months, Ashworth Enterprises has slapped a dozen injunctions on our current work projects."

"Injunctions?"

She said to rip it. Here it goes. Rip. Rip. Rip. "They allege that our work is shoddy and poses a threat to public safety. We've been court-ordered to cease and desist until we can prove otherwise."

"Any truth to the claims?"

"None at all, though Ashworth has managed to buy false witness—offering to purchase our clients' properties at above market value if they help stall our work. We'll eventually be cleared, but I'm afraid not in time to keep from going under."

"Why would Ashworth Enterprises want to see Murdock & Etting dissolve?"

He hesitated a moment, not sure how to answer her. As kids, they hadn't felt the conflict, being more interested in school, youth group, snowmobiling, riding their ATVs, and music. He knew bad blood existed between Big Mike and Robert's father, but teenagers rarely question life when their bellies are full and love encompasses them. Afghanistan brought Dwight's innocence to an end. Maybe Jolene still clung to hers.

Fiddlers Fling

"I'm not sure where the bad blood started between your father and Sean Ashworth. It's been going on for decades."

She reached down and skipped a pebble across the narrows.

"Their interference can't be simply revenge. Murdock & Etting is the only construction company in town, and a big employer. If the company folds, it would force even more unemployment and place a drain on the town's economy. No one wins. Including the Ashworths."

"My father said that the feud started after a jealous altercation over a woman."

Jolene's gaze met his, eyes wide. Anger or shock? "Are you saying this is Hatfield and McCoy stuff?"

Dwight sat on a boulder and invited Jolene to sit next to him. "Not that kind of feud, crossing state lines and involving extended family. I think it's simpler than that, but the impact is dividing Brookside into opposing viewpoints. All I know for sure is that Big Mike and a handful of businesses won't support the Ashworth political machine. I agree with your father on that score, and his influence still runs deep in a lot of Brookside circles. I'd bet the farm, if it were left, that politics is behind all of this."

"How so?"

"Big Mike believes your marrying an Ashworth is the same as a defection, a slap against everything he believes. Whatever bridge separates the families, the war ends when you say, 'I do' because Ashworth wins the final battle. They own his daughter."

Jolene laughed.

"What's so funny?"

"You are."

"I wasn't trying to be."

"In high school, you were always the quiet type. I never knew you were so articulate. Maybe you should run for councilman."

"I don't think so." Speaking in public was as painful as getting a tooth extracted. He couldn't put a sentence together except with Jolene. "I'll stick to hammering nails instead of spitting out words. Appreciate the compliment, though."

Jolene gazed into his eyes. "As for Robert, he has little involvement in the family business. Maybe, as his wife, I can change things. Help him see that monopoly is bad for the economy. Brookside was once a flourishing town."

"The operative word being 'once.'"

"It can be again. With the right leadership."

How could someone so annoyingly naïve be so beautiful? Love might be blind, but even the unsighted recognize a dangerous animal by its roar. "Do you seriously believe Robert's that noble?"

Jolene stood, her back arched, her glare piercing his cynicism. "Robert has his faults, but he's favorable toward small businesses. As a state senator, he'll be able to help Brookside compete in the larger economy."

"Do you hear yourself? They've got you, Jolene, just as your father feared. You're spouting more rhetoric than Alicia Davenport."

Her face reddened. "We're getting nowhere. Every time Robert's name pops up, we argue. Talk to me about these new contracts. How will they help?"

They resumed their walk. For now, he'd tell Jolene the facts and let her come up with her own conclusions. "The proposed contracts are for new buildings rather than renovating existing property, so the current injunctions wouldn't hinder us."

Still walking, she said, "I can see how a nursing home, a new school, a church, and a small housing development would be a huge boost to the town, as well as for Murdock & Etting."

Something large and brown crossed their path, and Jolene jumped. He caught her ... and his heart raced. He wanted to bring her closer, to kiss her, shout at her to forget Robert Ashworth. Instead, he helped her regain her balance.

"What was that thing?"

"Looked like a coyote."

"I forgot they run wild in the Adirondacks. Haven't seen one since that time we rode our ATVs over the back trails at the hunting lodge."

"I suppose some farmer will cut his lifespan short."

Jolene picked up a dried dandelion and blew the seeds into the wind. "The way of the world. Get in someone's way, dare to threaten their livelihood, and the beast comes out."

"Are you referring to the coyote, Robert, or your father?"

She smiled. "I don't know. Something's not adding up. If the new contracts would help Brookside, why wouldn't my father make sure they happen?"

"I can't answer that. Not only will the properties bring in badly needed cash for the village, but the project developers are homegrown investors."

"So are the Ashworths."

"That's true. However, Ashworth Enterprises already owns sixty percent of Brookside and is actively trying to increase their holdings." He'd come this far; no more tiptoeing around the truth. "These contracts would bring in jobs. More jobs means more spending. More spending means established businesses would prosper and be less dependent upon Ashworth Enterprises for loans and payouts. Right now, Murdock & Etting might very well be the wall that prevents Ashworth Enterprises from a complete takeover."

"But the Foundation raises a lot of money. The Ashworths have contributed millions toward social programs. How can you say they're all about themselves?"

"Are you so sure those fundraisers are totally about the needy? Have you ever asked yourself why organized crime would want to contribute to homeless shelters?"

She turned away. "No."

Dwight never claimed to be a philosopher or a scholar. This much he knew from simply observing how the world works. Since the dawn of time, powerful families often acquired their influence through questionable practices. While future generations might fight for the common man, the source of their political prowess continued to be mired in deceitful practices. Why did Jolene resist taking in the whole truth of her future in-laws? Dwight imagined reading biographies about the Kennedys was one thing, while realizing you are a breath away from becoming an addition to a seedy fortune quite another.

For her sake, for Brookside's sake, he'd held nothing back. The town's future might very well rest in the hands of a disillusioned heiress.

Jolene tried to concentrate on the beauty of an Adirondack spring, the wildflowers pushing their way through recently thawed ground, and rivers running sparkling clean, flushed of frozen debris. Neither spoke on the walk back to the house. She remembered many such strolls, her hand interlocked with Dwight's. The young girl still locked inside wanted to find comfort in the strength of his grasp.

Propriety trumped desire.

When they reached the house, Dwight got into his truck. "I'll see you tomorrow?"

"Maybe."

Jolene went back inside to say goodnight to Daddy. He sat at the kitchen table, eating a slice of her pie and a biscuit. "Forgot what a good cook you are, Jolene."

She relished his acknowledgement. "Thank you."

"Louise is a good cook too. Something you two gals have in common. Think I'll watch the news a bit. Probably fall asleep."

Dismissed. "I might as well take off. Good night. I'll see you tomorrow."

As she drove to the Ashworth mansion, worries and revelations curdled in her mind like sour milk. She entered the circular drive just as David made his way from the house. "I was concerned, ma'am, when I didn't hear from you. Glad you're back safe and sound. Mr. Ashworth sticks to a schedule, so I pretty much know when I need to be here to park the car for him."

"David, I'm quite capable of parking my own car. Don't tell Mr. Ashworth, but I know how to pump my own gas too. Just show me where I can leave my vehicle. That way I don't have to bother you. My schedule is pretty uncertain right now. You've got other things to tend to, I'm sure."

He paled. "If that's what you wish, ma'am. I don't care what time of day or night you need it. My orders are to make sure you get the proper assistance."

"Don't worry. I won't say a word to Mr. Ashworth. I like my independence, is all. I hope you'll understand."

David pointed to a multi-story garage jutting along the rear of the mansion. "It's a little easier to access if you take the back entrance to the estate, Miss Murdock. There's a private gas pump to the side of the garage." David wrote a series of letters and numbers on a piece of paper and handed it to her. "I only have one set of remotes, but there's a keypad on the pump and on the garage. Are you sure this is what you want? What if it rains?"

"I brought an umbrella. Please, David, don't worry."

He tipped his hat. "Yes, ma'am."

She parked the car, a rebel spirit rising.

Tomorrow she'd see about moving into her old bedroom. Two nights in this mausoleum were two nights too many.

Chapter Nine

Jolene turned on the bedside lamp. She scanned the room, feeling as if she'd been time-warped to late 18th-century France when detrimental extravagance prompted a revolution and cost royalty their heads. She could hear the queen's lack of compassion when she told the people who had no bread, "Let them eat cake," much like the cry of the privileged even today.

Unlike Marie Antoinette, Jolene cared that people suffered, which is why she earned a social-work degree. She wondered, though, if all her efforts at managing the Ashworth Foundation truly made a difference. Dwight's innuendo replayed in her mind. Were funds filtered from illegal sources through Ashworth coffers? The Ashworths donated millions. But in truth, what percentage of the money they raised actually went to charities? Or were those charities fronts for other purposes? Perhaps she should investigate the accounting procedures and examine the list of contributors. Was she inadvertently a part of a political scheme when she'd been promised a chance to do much good?

She rose and looked out the window. Not even a promise of daylight. No sense trying to go back to sleep. Dwight's reports of suspected subterfuge, of industrial attacks against Murdock & Etting, echoed non-stop. She dressed in jeans, tee, and flannel shirt, hardly grand-staircase attire, so unlike the ancestral Ashworth mistresses who graced the banisters with the latest Paris fashions. She turned and took the servants' stairwell. More fitting for this temporary dress code, and it was closer to the garage. If all went well, she'd spend the rest of her nights in her old room. At worst, only one last evening in Creepyland.

She reached her father's in less than ten minutes. This speeding habit of hers had to stop. Robert would be livid if she got a ticket, although he'd probably find a way to have her record expunged.

The house was dark. She opened the door. "Daddy?"

No answer, the now familiar drone of the television absent. He must be in his room. She longed to talk to him, to be more than just another person in his house—a person he tolerated for the moment. She took out biscuits and sausage gravy to heat when he came downstairs.

Too early to make phone calls, she grabbed a rag to wash the counter ... and stopped. The counters and floor gleamed as if newly scrubbed. When had Louise found time to clean? Must be something Jolene could do that was helpful.

The pantry might need straightening. She opened the door, eyeing a jar of canned pickles on the lower shelf. She remembered Daddy never liked homemade pickles, but she used to devour them whenever anyone brought over a can. She took out the jar. A gift from Louise?

Jolene struggled to pry the lid loose. She ran hot water over it and tried again; it still wouldn't budge. Determined to win one battle, she tapped the cover on the kitchen sink. Mistake. The jar slipped from her hand and splintered glass spewed across the counter, the briny contents collecting into a sticky puddle. She released a heavy sigh. "Just like the mess of my life," she announced to no one.

She mopped up her spill, then sat in a table chair, feeling the urge to sob but refusing the show of self-pity. No, she didn't crave pickles; she wanted answers—such as, what to do about Robert.

Three days ago, her future read like the last page of a romance novel. Now, thanks to Dwight, she found herself in the middle of the story possibly rewriting her preconceived happy-ever-after fairytale. She'd held no delusion that Robert modeled a perfect Prince Charming. He could be conceited, manipulative, and rude at times. Yet when in his arms, terror fled. He loved her. Or at least she'd thought so. Had she been wrong about that too?

Until yesterday, she believed Robert desired to faithfully represent the people who elected him. Yes, he'd been born into privilege. If the Ashworth millions had been gained through questionable moral means, she doubted they had involved themselves with anything illegal. She recalled the kings of Israel. Good sons had been born to evil parents. Should she assume Robert had anything less than honorable designs for Brookside simply because his father's money might be held in question? The Ashworths of years ago may have bent a few laws in their favor, but she wasn't marrying into a mob family.

Robert sometimes took her suggestions, at least where the Ashworth Foundation was concerned. In her place of influence, she'd been able to make significant contributions to dozens of charities, impacting thousands of lives for the better. If she married Robert, together they could right any ancestral wrongs. She'd be Robert's voice of reason, the clamor of goodwill in his rhetoric.

There. She'd reset her purpose.

The stairs creaked, and soon Daddy appeared in the kitchen, dressed in clean clothes and smelling of Irish Spring soap. He eyed the biscuits and sausage gravy on the stove. "Louise come over again?"

"I made breakfast for you."

"You're up mighty early."

"Couldn't sleep."

"Try warm milk before you go to bed."

"I'll do that."

He went into the den, turning on the television to *Fox and Friends*. Jolene lifted a notebook from her tote and added to her list of things she needed to accomplish before returning to Albany. The sooner she made arrangements for her father's care, the sooner she could resume her life by Robert's side.

She sent him a text: *arrangements progressing will call tonight.*

She went into the den. "Daddy, I have to go to the laundromat later. Want me to wash your linen for you?"

"Louise did it yesterday."

"When did she come over?"

"Right after the football game."

"That was after I left?"

"Yep."

Jolene checked the cupboards to make a shopping list. Everything had been reordered, organized by type of food and expiration date.

Fiddlers Fling

She looked under the sink. The cleaning supplies she'd bought had been replaced by different brands. Checking the storage bin on the back porch, she found the items tucked away in a box. She should be grateful someone had gone to all this trouble. Why, then, did she feel infringed upon?

She set the table for breakfast. "Daddy, everything's ready." He came back into the kitchen, sat down, and dug in, his hands exhibiting a very slight tremor upon extension. From booze withdrawal, or was his disease progressing? She wrote in her notebook again: *contact Doc Benson.* She needed to know exactly what was medically wrong. Some liver cancer was treatable. She could hope ... hope for more time with Daddy.

She sat across from her father. "How late did Louise stay?"

"Went home after the *Late, Late Show.*"

"Looks like she did a lot of cleaning. Nice she's willing to do so much for you."

He winked. "Woman thinks I'm her personal mission field. Besides, she insisted I clean the place up while you're here at least."

Jolene's eyes misted. Crazy way of showing he cared. "I'll be sure to tell her thank you."

"I plan on paying her. Don't want no charity."

"Would you mind if I stay in my old room until I go back to Albany? I'd like to visit you more often too."

He took a bite of biscuit. "It's not a fit place to sleep right now. But if you want to, go ahead. I never stopped ya from coming home."

What did she expect? A gushy "That's great"— and by some miracle, a hug?

"I know how to spackle and paint. I'll call Mattress Barn and have a bed sent over. It'll be fun to fix it up."

His expression went blank, yet he spoke with finality. "I'll pay for the stuff you need. I ain't broke. Won't have no Ashworth money going into this house."

"I have my own money from my job."

"Still Ashworth money as far as I'm concerned. You're my little girl. I always took good care of you, didn't I?"

"Yes, you did."

Talk of money gave her an open door to ask a few more questions. "Dwight said Sam Gooden's accounting firm manages most of the company transactions. Does he help with your personal accounts as well?"

Daddy met her gaze. "No worry on that score. I handle my own money." He walked to a drawer, pulled it open, and rummaged through its contents. "That checkbook was in this drawer yesterday when I paid the newspaper boy. I keep cash in that drawer too. Did you take it?"

"I haven't touched anything of yours without permission."

"Well, somebody took it."

"Maybe you moved it and forgot."

He slammed the drawer shut. "I don't forget about money. I tell you, Jolene, it ain't there, and I didn't move it. See for yourself."

She went through the drawer—no checkbook or cash but instead piles of overdue notices for utilities. "They're threatening to turn off your electricity."

"Those are old notices. I paid 'em last week."

"Sit back down and finish your breakfast. Let me see if I can find your checkbook." She pulled a kitchen chair over and searched the higher cupboards where her father used to keep things like fruit bowls and fancy dishes he never used. Gone were her mother's fine china and crystal, things promised to her when she married. A large white envelope leaned against the back of the cupboard.

"Is this what you're looking for?"

He threw it into the drawer. "A mystery to be sure. Well, it's where it belongs now."

She'd have to wait until he was out of sight before going over his register and the overdue notices in the drawer. She rejoined him at the table.

"Does anybody help you go over your bills when they come in?"

"I ran a multi-million dollar business. I think I know how to manage money."

He headed toward the porch, wobbling a little less. When he returned, he scanned the kitchen as if in a daze. "Where's the paper? I get a paper every day."

"I haven't seen one since I came. Are you sure the paperboy's still coming?"

"I paid somebody yesterday. Said they was the new paperboy."

Fiddlers Fling

He hadn't shown confusion until now. Professionally, she understood the ups and downs of mental deterioration. What if this was a sign of dementia? Should he live alone, even with help? She'd have to find this durable power of attorney Dwight claimed existed, and make certain everyone who needed a copy got one. She assumed Gordon Brockway, the company attorney, would have had it registered at the county clerk's office.

She added this task to her growing list.

Daddy tossed his paper plate and plasticware into the trash and hobbled into the den.

She grabbed his checkbook and perused the register. No entries. No way of knowing what he'd paid out of this account without going to the bank.

Still too early to make any phone calls. Might as well get started on cleaning her old room. She returned the checkbook, spending the next hour searching for a vacuum cleaner. None downstairs. She went upstairs. No vacuum there, either. If he didn't use one, maybe he stored it in the attic. She opened the door, pushing aside cobwebs, and climbed the sagging steps. She'd ask Dwight if he could send workmen to make repairs, starting with this dangerous staircase. She could handle the repairs in her room, but if she wanted to occupy it in a hurry, she'd need help. Once she gave the bank her copy of the power of attorney, she could deposit money into Daddy's account, then arrange for third-party notification on his utilities.

Fighting cobwebs, she reached the landing, only to be turned back by an overpowering, unrecognizable scent that captured her breath. She went back downstairs, giving up the chase for a vacuum. She'd buy one before she tried those steps again. Or maybe Louise knew where it was.

Jolene dug out the piece of napkin with Louise's phone number and glanced at the clock. Almost eight. Louise answered on the first ring.

"Louise, this is Jolene Murdock."

"Are you calling from Michael's?"

"Yes. First of all, thank you for your work yesterday."

"I don't mind at all."

"Daddy feels like he's taking advantage of your goodness. I agree. We'd like to officially hire you as his housekeeper."

"I'd do it for nothing, but someone hired me yesterday."

"Dwight?"

78

"No. A lady named Alicia something or other. Said she was a friend of your fiancé's and asked if I'd be willing to take care of Michael so's you could get back to Albany."

Jolene sat down. Heat surged, and nausea threatened to make her vomit. Shouldn't she have been asked before anyone else hired help for her father? Although she shouldn't be surprised. Robert might not be aware, either. Alicia invented the word *maverick*. She did her own thing when and how she wanted, beyond Ashworth suspicion.

"That Alicia woman gave me lots of money and said it would be a help to you and to Michael. I'd do anything to help Michael. So, I agreed."

Jolene cleared her throat to keep from screaming obscenities at Alicia's interference. "My father would be livid if he knew someone else paid you on his behalf. He'd view it as charity. From now on, your pay will come from us."

"If it's the only way Michael will let me help him, I'll agree to it. But cash only."

She ventured the question, trying hard not to sound accusatory. "I noticed the cleaning products I bought had been moved to storage and different products are now under the sink."

"No mystery. I'm fussy about what I use to clean, especially if I'm getting paid to do work."

"No, that's okay. Use what you prefer. Make a list for me of what you need and the brands you want, and I'll make sure the house is supplied."

"I didn't buy them with my money. That Alicia woman gave me a hundred dollars for whatever, so I figured I'd buy stuff for the house. I didn't want her money."

Robert was about to get an earful. "One other thing, do you know where my father's vacuum cleaner is?"

"Did you check the attic?"

"Couldn't get past the odor."

"I'll clean the attic tomorrow. I was gonna bring over the mops and things I bought. Your father's brooms and such are in awful shape."

Who was that accommodating without motive, even for a neighbor? Did Louise have some hidden agenda? Jolene blew out her agitation in one long exhale. "I have my father's power of attorney, Louise. Promise me you won't accept any offers from anyone else. I'll pay you whatever you'd like to do the job."

"If that's what Michael wants."

"You mentioned you prefer cash. I'll still need your Social Security number for legality's sake. Any reason why I shouldn't ask for it?"

"No, none. Just like to keep things simple. If it was anybody else but Michael, I wouldn't bother."

"Sorry if I seemed annoyed for a moment. I wasn't angry with you."

"Glad for that. I'll see you this afternoon."

Next Jolene called Robert, but his phone went to voice mail. She left a message. "Was it your idea to have Alicia make care arrangements for my father behind my back? Don't ever let it happen again."

At the least, Louise did care about Daddy and probably would be there for him when Jolene returned to Albany. She should be grateful for the help, not jealous.

On to other things. Jolene called Nursing Services. After a series of instructions from the automated answering device, a female voice came on the line. "This is Loren," she announced, her tone friendly.

"At last, a person."

Loren offered a soft laugh. "We hear that a lot. Sign of the times, I guess. How may I help you?"

"I'd like to arrange home care for my father, Mike Murdock."

"Our agency is familiar with your father. We received a referral from Mr. Murdock's physician. However, so far he's refused our services ... on three separate home visits. The third time he wouldn't let us in."

"I have his durable power of attorney."

"If you're there, we'll attempt another evaluation. I must warn you, though, if he's still uncooperative, we may not be able to provide care in the home. Have you thought about a nursing home?"

Jolene tried to imagine her father in a residential care facility, the nearest one over twenty-five miles from Brookside, far away from everyone he knew. Without visitors or constant stimulation, he'd die of loneliness before the cancer took him. "I'd like to see what I can do for him at home before I go that route."

"Someone will be there about two o'clock to do an assessment, then we'll take it from there. Does he need housekeeping services too, or are you able to do that for him?"

"I've hired a neighbor, Louise Fournier. I don't plan on staying in town more than a few more days. If I can arrange care for him, I'll be returning to Albany."

A hitch in the nurse's voice brought alarm. "Louise Fournier is not on our list of approved housekeepers."

"My father refuses anyone else."

"I understand. That's your private matter. We can put in a personal-care aide to see to his hygiene, if he accepts one. You need to know, however, that state guidelines require the patient to have a primary caregiver."

"I should have thought of that. I'm a social worker and well aware of our convoluted health-care laws. I'll arrange for a primary caregiver to act in my stead when I return to Albany. In the meantime, I'll assume that role. And I do plan frequent visits."

"What kind of insurance does your father have?"

As a human services professional, she had never given thought to how intrusive these questions might be for families under duress. One thing to be the questioner and quite another to be the one required to answer. "I don't know. I'll pay for whatever isn't covered."

"Most homecare isn't covered at all unless your father has long-term home health insurance or Medicaid."

She hadn't expected government help, nor would Daddy accept it.

"And your father's too young for Medicare. Only fifty-two?"

A burn, like anger, made her twinge. Unfair that her father wouldn't live to see the completion of his sixth decade.

"I'll pay for whatever he needs."

"Homecare is very expensive. If a patient needs a lot of care, services can end up costing more than a nursing home and not be as efficient."

Would now be a good time to drop Robert's name? She disliked people who wielded their influence for selfish gain. But if it helped her father, she'd throw Robert's name around like confetti.

"I'm engaged to Robert Ashworth. I'm sure we'll have the resources to meet my father's needs."

Loren hesitated. "We don't dispense care based on who a patient may or may not be related to. We neither discriminate nor give preferential treatment to self-pay patients."

An expected response. But experience had already taught Jolene that privilege still caught the best opportunities.

Reality hit. How would she pay for homecare? Her token wages were direct deposited. Since her engagement, the Ashworths gave her a generous allowance, more than enough for her increased spending habits, especially since she had no housing expenses or bills of any kind. But given Robert's insistence she send her father to a nursing home, would he be willing to help fund expensive home care? A housekeeper was one thing, but an entourage of nurses, aides, and assistive therapists would prove to be very costly.

No. If Robert refused to help, she'd find a way. Family was family.

She called Dwight. He'd probably be on a job site or at the office, but she hoped he'd answer. "Murdock & Etting."

"Why so official? Don't you check caller ID?"

"Sometimes. What's up?"

"Where are you?"

"At a job site. Just about finished."

"I called Nursing Services. They'll be here at two. I have a huge favor to ask."

"Ask."

"I can't arrange for Daddy's homecare unless he has a primary caregiver."

"And you hoped I'd be that person."

"You're like family, as far as my father's concerned."

"I've tried to do things for him, but he's been very uncooperative. I don't think that'll change once you go back to Albany."

"I'm not so sure, Dwight. I wouldn't say he's pleasant to me, but Louise has been able to make a lot of headway. I wonder, though ... "

"Wonder what?"

Jolene heard her paranoia even before she spoke the words. "Can she be trusted? What do you know about her?"

"Not a lot. My father rented to the Fourniers before I came back from Afghanistan. She's a good tenant. Always pays her rent on time. Cash."

"And that doesn't seem odd to you?"

"I suppose our generation relies on credit and debit cards. But a lot of folks, especially here in Brookside, prefer doing business the old fashioned way—trust and a handshake. Doesn't mean she's dishonest. You're far too suspicious."

Should she clue Dwight on Alicia's arrangement? No. Dwight had enough reasons already to distrust the Ashworths ... Alicia too. "You're right. And since Daddy won't accept any other help, I should take advantage of Louise's willingness. But I'd still feel better if someone supervised her work."

"By someone, you mean me?"

"I know it's asking a lot—"

"Of course I will. I should warn you, though. You may get a lot of calls to come to the rescue."

"For Daddy or for you?"

Chapter Ten

Except for the work at Big Mike's house, the Daltons' addition and back porch would be Murdock & Etting's final project ... unless the contracts were signed. Dwight drove the last nail into the pressurized plank. He gazed upward, enjoying the view overlooking a series of stunted mountains.

Local history claimed what was now the Dalton estate had been a makeshift fortress built by settlers as protection against raids during the French and Indian War. Legend said a Dalton ancestor defected from the British Empire during the War of Independence and fought for the patriots, turning over large parcels of land to encourage the town's settlement in 1807. Dwight chewed his lower lip with the thought he might have to leave a town so rich in history.

Mahoney handed Dwight a bottle of water. "Pretty scenery around these parts."

Dwight pointed toward the east. "My father and Big Mike owned a lot of the land over there. Most of it's been sold off."

"Life's like that, I guess."

"How's that?"

"Seems nothing much stays the same since Adam and Eve got tossed out of Eden."

Dwight's cell rang and he flipped it open. Fernando Gomez. "Yeah, talk to me, Fernando."

Through broken English, Fernando apologized that he must put in his resignation.

Fiddlers Fling

Dwight ground his jaws. "Hate to see you leave us, *amigo*."

"I have other job starting tomorrow."

"Sorry I haven't been able to keep you busy enough. Where will you be working, if I can ask?"

"I have offer to build sheds—"

"You don't have to say it, Fernando. I know Ashworth's been wooing our crew with other employment to remodel his businesses."

"I need the work, Mister Etting."

"I understand."

Fernando made the seventh worker to bail in the last month. At this rate, once the contracts were signed, the company would be too shorthanded to begin in time to stave off bankruptcy. *"Buena suerte, mi amigo."* After wishing the man well, he ended the call.

Mahoney wiped his brow with a soiled bandana. "Let me guess. Fernando?"

"Yep. That means his brother is likely to quit soon too. Wherever one goes, the other follows."

"Kinda like us."

"Yeah."

"Did Jolene get her father to sign the contracts yet?"

"No. She promised to sign on her father's behalf if he continues to refuse. Tell ya, Jack, money's just about gone. Won't blame you if you want to quit. This isn't Afghanistan, and Brookside isn't your war. I can't keep asking you to work for no wages."

Mahoney laughed. "Way I figure, things will either get better or worse. If the business goes belly up, I'll apply for unemployment. If things pick up, well ... I like being busy."

"Can't argue with you there."

"Besides, I'd rather work for nothing than hang around the house all day. Nissie will make me a honey-do list a mile long. You know I can't cook—you've tasted my meatloaf."

"Pure poison. I see your point."

Mahoney transferred his tools from his belt to the nearby chest. "I'm okay for a couple more months, and the contracts should come in by then. Besides, like I said, I've got a few music gigs lined up. You could join me, you know. I don't have a keyboard yet."

"What kind of gigs?"

"A wedding, a retirement party, and six weekends at Josey's."

"I'll skip the bar scene if you don't mind, but count me in on the others."

"Deal."

Dwight stood, took his tools out of his belt, and handed them to Mahoney to store in the chest. Dwight sighed, deep and long. Could he pass it off as simple tiredness? "Warm afternoon."

Mahoney latched the chest. "I think there's more to that sigh than the heat."

Never could fool the man. "I thought I was doing a good thing for both her and Big Mike when I convinced Jolene to come to Brookside. Looks like I've complicated her life more than helped it."

"If she's engaged to an Ashworth, she knows complicated pretty well. You're probably not to blame if her mind's in a whirl."

"She has tough decisions to make where Big Mike's concerned. I've seen an improvement in him since Louise has been helping, and even more in the last couple of days. Maybe Jolene's coming home put a little spark back in him. Doesn't change the fact he's dying. Might have been better for her to stay in Albany and put her father in a nursing home near her. We could have managed the paperwork by mail or fax."

"You had no choice but to let her know about Big Mike's condition. She chose to come to Brookside." Mahoney raised his left brow. "Or did you have some other reason for calling her? Maybe you hoped she'd dump the fiancé and fall back into your arms?"

"Not really." Or maybe so. Perhaps a part of him wanted her to stay in Brookside, partner up with him, become the next generation of Murdock & Etting. What if God had a different plan? Perhaps her destiny was to be an Esther, brought to the King's palace to save Brookside in a way Dwight hadn't thought possible. If so, he was wrong to hound heaven with the hope she'd be free to marry him.

Mahoney swept the sawdust from the newly built porch.

Dwight picked up the tool chest and headed toward the truck, Mahoney close to his heels and carrying the broom. "Ever think that if the company bankrupts, Murdock & Etting would be under Ashworth's control? Truthfully, Dwight, I don't want them signing my paychecks."

"They wouldn't because they'd probably clean house and hire illegals to avoid dealing with a union. I keep telling myself Brookside is better off if we stand against an Ashworth monopoly. I have to admit, I'm not that noble. Truth is, I like being my own boss. All I want is to make an honest living and maybe provide an opportunity for others to do the same."

Mahoney opened the truck hatch. "I thought Councilman Richards was trying to get our injunctions lifted. According to the paper, he'd like to see the new projects forge ahead."

"The mayor too. If we can hang on long enough—"

Mahoney's phone chimed. "It's a text from Nissie."

"Wants more pizza?"

Mahoney's grin nearly split his face. "Nope. Baby's on its way. Guess we'd better get moving. She's taking a cab to the hospital. Will you drop me off?"

"Sure. I'll wait with you. Might have to dart off for a bit, though. Jolene wants me to be there when the nurse visits. Won't take long for him to refuse and put poor Jolene right back at square one."

Dwight loaded the tool chest, and Mahoney slid the broom into the bay. "I keep praying, asking God to take care of things."

"The business or Jolene?"

"Both."

Chapter Eleven

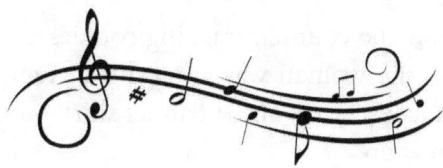

Dwight scanned the hospital waiting room, rose and paced, pulled between his promise to Jolene and his promise to Mahoney to wait it out with him. Only Mahoney was with Nissie in the labor room, and Dwight had been relegated to the lobby. Nothing he could do for Mahoney here.

A nurse popped into the waiting area, and Dwight called her over. "Any word on Mrs. Mahoney?"

The nurse smiled. "You must be Mr. Mahoney's friend. He was worried you'd get antsy here."

Just then Dwight's cell rang. Mahoney's voice started in before Dwight could even say hello. "Look, Nissie won't deliver for a few hours yet. Go on ahead to Jolene's. She probably needs you more than I do right now. Everything's going well, here. We're playing cards between contractions."

"Ten-four, Buddy."

Did Jolene really need him? If Mahoney only knew the Jolene Dwight knew—a woman so independent she waged war against herself.

He was in his car and headed away from the hospital in a matter of minutes. He despised being late and didn't want to disappoint Jolene, either. He pushed the pedal to the floor, careened a few turns, and breathed relief when he pulled into the driveway, getting out of the truck nearly instantaneously with putting it in park.

He checked his watch as he opened the door. Two on the dot. Not late. Fashionably punctual. The aroma of freshly baked cookies greeted him. Louise's or Jolene's? He remembered how Jolene liked to cook. She swore up and down she hated any kind of housework, but she was almost as handy in the kitchen as she was with a power saw.

He headed toward the kitchen but stopped when he saw his reflection in the mirror. His cap sported a huge stain, his tee was drenched with perspiration. What a sight. Hardly a look for *Cosmopolitan*. He should have taken the time to change after he left the hospital, even though he would have been late. Well, "tough beans," as Dad always said. This was Dwight Etting, a carpenter, and carpenters get sweaty. No use putting on airs for the Princess.

Jolene leaned over the counter, stacking cookies on a tray, her back to him. Front or back, the woman was an eyeful of temptation. Today she wore a pair of plain jeans, a tee, and a flannel shirt—a model's bearing no matter what she threw on.

He snuck up behind her and grabbed a fresh chocolate chip cookie. She turned, her face clean of pricey makeup, free to glow with natural beauty. Not like Alicia Davenport who couldn't go into Home Depot without two-hours of primping.

"Worried you weren't going to show."

"I always keep my promises. I'm here and on time. Had to leave Mahoney at the hospital. His wife's in labor."

"Everything okay?"

"Seems to be. I'll check when I get done here. I didn't have time to change."

"The nurse isn't coming to evaluate you." She leaned back. "You're fine."

He grabbed another cookie. "These are delicious. Yours or Louise's?"

"Mine. Don't take any more. They're for the nurse when she gets here." She put three bags of Lipton tea, Big Mike's favorite, into an antique-looking pot. "I found this stuck in a corner cupboard where my mother's old china had been stored. Daddy must have overlooked it when he got rid of all her dishes. They weren't fancy, but it was the only thing of my mother's he kept. He promised they'd be mine when I started a home of my own." Her eyes moistened. "Guess he decided an Ashworth wouldn't appreciate them."

"Maybe he still has them stored somewhere. Did you ask him?"

She sighed. "No. I was afraid of the answer. Silly to let all that bother me, isn't it?"

"Not at all."

She leaned against the counter, the snug fit of her jeans stoking desire. He looked away, keeping his gaze anywhere but on Jolene. "Big Mike's temper is no secret. He might cuss sometimes or put his fist through a wall. I remember how he used to pound the daylights out of a two-by-four when he got agitated. But I can't believe he'd deliberately hurt his only child by getting rid of something as precious to her as her mother's china."

"I've been thinking a lot about my mother, wishing I'd had a chance to know her. She died soon after I was born. As I got older, a lot of people said I looked like her."

"Big Mike used to keep a photo of her in the office. And yes, you do look like her, especially today."

"Are the photos still there?"

He hadn't thought it strange until now. "No."

"Maybe I'm being too paranoid, but it seems as if my father has systematically removed all traces of me from his life—ATVs, trophies, books, photo albums ... even my fiddle. Everything. I never thought I'd miss the things I left behind. And I didn't ... until I came back. Does he hate me that much?"

Her expressed heartache tugged at his desire for her. Forgetting propriety, he pulled her into an embrace as he lifted her chin. She gazed at him with wet blue eyes, like oceans, deep and wide, vibrant, pristine ... and sans makeup. "Your father doesn't hate you. If he thought you were never coming back, why keep them in plain sight?"

Jolene pulled away and walked toward the window. "True. But everything? Didn't you keep some of your father's things after he died?"

"A few pictures and his pipe."

"You don't smoke."

"Neither did my father. But the pipe belonged to my grandfather. Dad never used tobacco. He'd sit in a rocker, put the thing in his mouth, and look like he was going off someplace. Only when the Pats played."

Jolene smiled. "I remember he was a huge Patriots fan, and my father rooted for the opposite team just to goad Ken. Probably the only thing he and Daddy argued about. It surprises me you kept that pipe. I don't remember you being the sentimental type."

Her tone was flat. So much for their tender moment.

"War makes you see the world differently, especially when you're not sure if you're coming back home standing up, in a wheelchair, or in a casket."

Fiddlers Fling

She picked up the tray and teapot, and Dwight followed her to the table. "My father got rid of my things out of spite, not practicality. He'll never forgive me. He tolerates me because I'm family. I'd hoped we could manage some kind of relationship other than a cold truce. Silly me."

She swayed back into the kitchen, returning with two hands full of coffee mugs, then set them on the table next to the platter. "He didn't even keep the teacups that go with the pot. These mugs will have to do."

"She's a nurse, not the president."

They both laughed, and Jolene dared to smile. "I'm glad you're here, Dwight. In some ways, you know Daddy better than I do. The father I remember was strong, decisive, cared about Brookside, loved his work, loved his daughter, and loved the Lord."

"The old Big Mike is still in there ... somewhere."

She returned to the kitchen and came back with leftover apple pie, putting the few remaining slices on the platter with the cookies.

"Yours?"

Her cheeks reddened. "Yes. Daddy prefers Louise's though."

"You don't seem to like her much."

Jolene pursed her lips. "The question isn't whether I like Louise or not. The fact is, he refuses to accept anyone else's help. She seems nice enough, but something about her unsettles me—a little too accommodating, if you ask me. Did you know Alicia Davenport hired her the day I arrived? Without my knowledge or permission, I might add."

Dwight took off his cap and hung it on the chair knob. "Why would I know that? Now who's paranoid? Maybe your fiancé wanted to do something nice for you." *Yeah, right.* Jolene would see through her old boyfriend's defending her fiancé, though he didn't blame her for disliking Alicia. That club numbered over half of Brookside, women primarily. Most of the men weren't interested in her personality. "Louise has a big heart."

They both jumped at the thud.

"What was that?"

She looked toward the ceiling. "Louise is cleaning the attic. I told her it could wait until tomorrow. She insisted on investigating the odor before it worked its way downstairs. She's all decked out like a HazMat worker. She insisted on cleaning out my old bedroom today too. They're delivering a new bed later this afternoon. I'm moving in, holes in the walls or not. Don't want to spend another night at Hill House."

He laughed, straight from the gut. "That eerie?"

"Not that, exactly. It's too eighteenth-century, like Louis XVI's ghost frequents the place."

Dwight remembered night strolls when they'd talk about the older homes in Brookside, imagine who built them, and wonder aloud what happened to past owners. Sometimes they'd go to the library or the House of History and research Brookside's upper crust. The Ashworths were the only Brookside wealth to survive the fall of the millionaires after the market crashed.

Dwight missed those adventures. Weren't many girls who challenged him toward academics other than what he was forced to learn in school. He hadn't been to a library since he and Jolene broke up.

"I'm hoping to return to Albany in a few days, but I plan on visiting as often as possible."

Dwight resisted the urge to pound the table. As an observer of human behavior, he believed most stubbornness stemmed from a natural inclination to resist the unpleasant. Stubbornness defined a Murdock, independent of conscious thought—an inbred, dogged craziness. "I can't believe you're still going to marry that jerk. Not after everything we talked about."

Jolene's chin firmed—her cheeks puffed in defiance. "Something my father would say. Both of you are so blinded by mistrust you can't see Robert's good points. He'll be a fantastic senator. And the Ashworth Foundation channels thousands into Brookside youth activities like the YMCA and Little League, as well as drug-rehab programs. In fact, Robert has proposed building a youth behavioral center so troubled youth will be nearer their families instead of having to be admitted to city facilities and thrown in with hardened street thugs."

Dwight growled. "I doubt he plans on giving the building contract to Murdock & Etting."

Jolene balled her fists, Murdock ire written on her face. "Is that all you care about?"

"Of course not. But I have the feeling the idea is more yours than Robert's. Am I right?"

She sat and crossed her arms. "It doesn't matter who came up with the idea—the important thing is that it happens. Don't you see? Robert and I make a good team."

Fiddlers Fling

Dwight pushed the chair against the table, harder than necessary. "I can't stop you, and neither can your father. I've tried to be understanding ... tried to believe that perhaps God has a plan in all this ... that I've been judgmental ... jealous. I've asked the Lord to give me peace that you and I are over. But with every fiber of my being, I'm convinced that if you marry Robert Ashworth, you'll live to regret it."

She uncrossed her arms. "I don't think so. But if I do, I do. I've learned to live with a lot of regret. I'll adjust. We all make mistakes. Life goes on."

"If you're referring to us, it's not too late to start over."

But it is too late, Dwight. How could she make him understand she couldn't go back to him, whether she married Robert or not. Dwight couldn't be in her future. Yet, this man before her—sweaty, with dirty carpenter pants and stubble—pulled at her will. How easy to forget she was engaged and to remember how she and Dwight used to be. No amount of regret could change what she did, nor could any amount of good works atone for her sin against him.

He took her hand, pulled her close, and kissed her. She longed to surrender to him once again as she had before. But regret bubbled, bringing her back from the abyss. She'd ask him to leave, but she owed Dwight friendship—if not for herself, for Murdock & Etting ... for Daddy. She pushed away. "No, Dwight. My path is clear."

Chapter Twelve

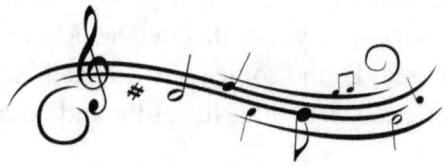

Jolene sighed with relief at the doorbell's ring, a rescue from another weak moment. Dwight stared at her like a kid whose ice-cream cone lay splattered on the pavement. What had he expected? That once he kissed her she'd dump Robert, stay in Brookside, and take up where they'd left off? Impossible. Any hope of that happening died with the abortion.

She knew now that he thought he still loved her. What would he think of her if he knew she'd killed his child?

She could easily love the Dwight she'd come to know over the past few days, in some ways like the boy who went to war ... yet different. Kinder, gentler. The more time they spent together, the more yesterday's ghosts whittled away her hope for tomorrow. If only she could discard regret as easily as Daddy had her mother's china.

Jolene opened the door. A slightly obese woman with shoulder- length dark hair and raccoon eyes stared at her. "Zoey Carmichael?"

"So you recognize me. Didn't think you would. I'm about a hundred pounds heavier than I was in high school."

She smiled and ignored the obvious announcement. "Come in. Dwight's in the kitchen."

"Dwight Etting?"

Jolene nodded and led the way, anxious to see the look on his face when he saw this nurse. She knew about Zoey's flirtations, though Dwight tried to excuse them. No need to be jealous. He never reciprocated, but no matter his protests to the contrary, what man didn't secretly enjoy being the object of any woman's affection?

If nothing else the interchange might provide some much-needed amusement. When Zoey entered the kitchen, Dwight's bugged eyes met hers. She smiled, glancing back and forth between Dwight and Jolene. "Well, well, well. Dwight Etting and Jolene Murdock in the same room once again."

"Hello, Zoey," he squeaked, his cheeks as red as the kitchen curtains Louise had put up earlier.

Zoey laughed. "Get over yourself, Dwight. My crush on you ended about the time it started. Found someone who liked me back."

Jolene tilted her head, laughing inwardly and waited for Dwight to extricate himself.

Zoey looked back at Jolene. "Did you know I had a wicked crush on Dwight during our senior year?"

Yes! "He never mentioned it."

"I'm not surprised. I kissed him after the homecoming football game, and he near had a heart attack. Isn't that right, Dwight?"

His face deepened three more shades of red.

"He only had eyes for you, Jolene. Surprised you two didn't end up together. Everyone thought you would."

Now it was Jolene's turn to blush. If only turning back the calendar were possible. "What about you, Zoey? So you're a nurse now. That's great. Where did you go to school?"

"Columbia. Met my husband there. We lived in New York City until six months ago." Her voice dropped a notch. "Getting a divorce."

The Zoey she remembered. All chatter, willing to give up the most intimate details of her life.

Jolene bit her lower lip, fighting to hold back the sarcasm that had been her high school stock-and-trade. The girl she used to be would have given Zoey the boot and called Nursing Services, demanding they send someone else. What happened to that strong-willed personality? Years with the Ashworths had taught Jolene to be less outwardly abrasive, to *use* rather than confront.

Zoey took out a clipboard filled with paperwork. "I saw your engagement announcement in the paper. How did a Brookside girl manage to snag Robert Ashworth?"

Don't bite, Jolene. "The wedding is scheduled for seven weeks from Saturday. So you see why I really need to get back."

Zoey nodded. "You could put your father into a nursing home in Albany to keep a close eye on him. I believe the Ashworths own several, so placement shouldn't be a problem."

"I would prefer my father stay in his own home as long as possible. I wondered about hospice, although he doesn't need a lot of personal care at this time."

"As long as his prognosis is less than two years, we can slip him into the program, monitor his progress, and put in services as needed ... *if* he'll accept."

"When do you want to see him?"

"No time like the present."

"He's in the den."

"See if you can get him to come into the kitchen, and I can evaluate his ADLs."

Jolene explained for Dwight's sake. "Activities of Daily Living— things like ambulation, transferring from chair to a stand, etc. I think he might benefit from occupational therapy."

Zoey wrote on one of her forms. "You're getting ahead of yourself, Jolene. I need to speak with your father before we start planning the rest of his life."

Dwight sat, wishing he'd stayed at the hospital. Even if he was relegated to the lobby, at least he could be reading a magazine instead of being embarrassed to death. Jolene headed for the den, leaving Dwight alone with Zoey. "Sorry to hear about your divorce."

"Found out he was gay. He wants to marry his lover."

No good way to respond to that. He shifted in his chair, the conversation going from uncomfortable to out-and-out excruciating.

Zoey scribbled information on one of the forms. "Why are you here, Dwight? This doesn't have anything to do with the business, does it?"

"Yes and no. Jolene asked me to serve as primary caregiver—if that's the right term—when she goes back to Albany."

Zoey met his gaze. "I'd say you're hoping she doesn't go back."

"And I'd say that's wrong. If she's happy with Robert Ashworth ... well ... I wish her all the best."

Her eyes twinkled with mischief when she answered. "Methinks the man doth protest too much."

Jolene returned, Daddy trailing behind, while Zoey cast an analytical glance their way. Dwight stood, his hands in his pockets, staring at Zoey as she thumbed through her stack of clipped paperwork and pulled out a five-page evaluation form.

Eyeing the cookies and tea, Daddy stopped at the archway. "What's going on? I feel like I'm being ambushed."

"This is Zoey Carmichael. Dwight and I knew her in high school."

He helped himself to a chocolate chip cookie as he glanced around the room. "Nobody else wants any?"

Dwight reached for one. "Think I will." He took a big bite. "Apparently life with the Ashworths hasn't ruined your baking skills, Jolene."

Daddy scowled. "Thought Louise made these. But Jolene used to be a pretty fair cook. Probably just as good."

Jealousy reared again, but she pushed it away and offered another tidbit of information. "Zoey's a nurse."

"Don't need a nurse." Daddy staggered slightly, then steadied himself against the table.

Zoey leaned forward. "Jolene tells me you have a woman who comes over to help with your housework."

He nodded. "Louise."

"Louise Fournier?"

A siren of concern blared. Jolene answered for her father. "Yes. Why do you ask?"

"She used to work for us."

"Used to?"

Zoey shifted her gaze toward the paperwork. "I'm sorry. I can't say anything more than that."

"Daddy, I have to get back to Albany soon. I want to make sure you have someone to look after you ... someone Dwight and I can trust."

"Louise'll do that. You can leave whenever you have a mind to. Nice to meet you, Zoey, but I don't need any help. Managing just fine." He ambled toward the sink, threw in the rest of his cookie, and wobbled back to the den.

Zoey put the paperwork back in the tote. "I expected he'd be resistive. There's really nothing we can do. You have help. If I were you, I'd start the process for a nursing home. Soon. Given his diagnosis, you can expect a rapid decline within the next month, perhaps sooner."

"That's it?"

"If the patient refuses, our hands are tied. Sorry I couldn't be more helpful."

As she showed Zoey to the front door, Jolene swallowed the tears wanting to escape. When she returned to the kitchen, Dwight pulled her into a hug, and she accepted his comfort. "When you called Saturday, everything seemed so simple. I'd come home, make a few calls, and *voila!*"

He stroked her hair. "God has a plan, Jolene. He'll show us in his time."

Us, Dwight had said. She trembled, and before she could stop him, his lips met hers. She felt his want for her, and she let him know she wanted him too, before finding the will to pull away. *This can't happen. Not now— not ever.* "No, Dwight."

"I'm sorry, Jolene. I lost control."

Not the first time.

"I won't let it happen again."

"You better go."

"I don't want to leave you like this. I think we need to talk."

"About what?"

"What do you think?"

"I'm still marrying Robert."

A scream from the attic sent them scurrying upstairs, Big Mike ambling behind them. Louise met them on the landing holding two dead squirrels. "Looks like I found the source of the stink."

Father, daughter, and Dwight joined Louise for a quartet of laughter.

Chapter Thirteen

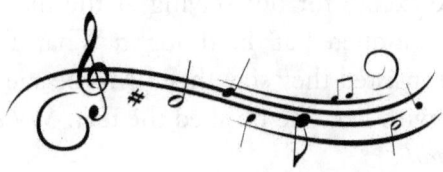

Jolene waved the Mattress Barn deliverers inside just as Dwight was about to leave. "I can put that up for you," he said, strutting like a peacock toward the stairwell.

"You forget I know how to do these things. Bet I could do it faster too. But thanks for the offer. Besides, you should get back to the hospital to see how Nissie's doing."

She shooed him out the door, then went upstairs and assembled her bed. She'd have to go to the mansion and pack up, after which she'd stop at the discount store to purchase sheets and a comforter. Patching the holes could wait as long as she had something to sleep on other than the floor.

She went into the den, but Daddy was on his way to the kitchen. "So you're really going to stay here?"

"At least until I go back to Albany. As I promised, I'll be a frequent visitor."

He nodded. "Any more of those cookies left?"

"They're still on the counter."

"Good." Volumes of hope edged the short exchange.

"I'll be back in a few minutes. I have to go to the Ashworth estate and gather up what's there. Do you want anything at the store?"

"I'm good. Louise is bringing over supper in a bit."

But, of course!

Fiddlers Fling

Jolene searched for any sign of David. He'd either gone home or was busy somewhere else on the estate. She left the car running in the circular drive, expecting to be only a few minutes.

The house creaked in its emptiness. She hurriedly packed her suitcase, putting the few purchases she'd made into a tote, and practically ran out the door.

Silly to be frightened.

She sent Robert a text. *Moving into my old room.* Perhaps she should give some plausible excuse for not staying at the mansion other than it felt too creepy. She shuddered at the thought: What if Robert decided to visit Brookside and insisted they stay there? Maybe she wouldn't dislike it so much if he were with her. She finished the text. *So I can be more readily available to help Daddy.*

She tapped send, then eased out of the driveway, ready to outrun any ethereal creature that followed her. She glanced into the rearview mirror as a Lincoln Town Car pulled up into the circular drive and David got out of the car. Not a vehicle any of the Ashworths normally drove. Had someone else been staying at the house? David indicated Jolene had been alone. Why would he lie about that?

If she purchased the comforter from Seconds 'R Us, she could be in and out of the store within minutes. She perused the linen section, opting for a paisley bed set, a pattern she'd favored as a teenager. Maybe being home after so long made her feel like a kid again.

With a sense someone was watching her, she neared the linen aisle. She turned quickly and saw Alicia Davenport as she ducked behind the pillow display. Was she following Jolene again? What excuse would be offered this time? No milk in this store.

Jolene pushed the cart away, then double backed. Alicia stood in the middle of the aisle. Jolene used her most threatening glare. "Why are you following me?"

Alicia smacked her lips and placed her hands on her hips. "If you must know, I came in here to pick up a birthday gift for my secretary."

"Are you buying her bedsheets?"

"I was taking a short cut to the cosmetic department. She likes Chantilly. Of course, not a scent I'd choose for myself."

"Of course not. If you don't stop following me, I'm warning you, I'll get a restraining order."

Her cackle sounded like something out of a B-rated horror film, an Elvira in white Nordstrom capris. "I don't think so. You have no proof. And I've made no threats."

"I'm serious. Stop following me." She left Alicia in the dust of a sprint to the check-out. Jolene paid for her purchases and rushed back to the house at speeds a NASCAR driver would find intimidating.

Louise and Daddy sat at the kitchen table, enjoying a tuna-noodle casserole.

Louise smiled. "Saved you some, dear."

Jolene glanced at the table, glad to see the dinnerware she'd bought being used.

"Hope you don't mind we used your plates."

"I bought them for all of us."

Louise served a portion of the casserole and put it on the table. "Sit and eat, dear."

Daddy nodded. "It's real good." He took the last bite from his plate, but instead of bringing it to the sink and going back into the den, he stayed at the table. "Louise and I were thinking of going out to a movie. Want to go?"

Perhaps she should. Get her mind off Alicia. *If only murder were legal.*

Daddy and Louise looked into each other's eyes. Was this a date?

If so, they didn't need a chaperone.

"You two go on. I want to take this comforter I bought upstairs and settle into my room."

Daddy shrugged. "Suit yourself."

Louise picked up the dishes and put them in the sink. "I'll wash these when we get back. Just cover the casserole and stick it in the fridge when you're finished."

They left with Jolene more curious about Louise than ever. Why stir a romance with a dying man? Was she a gold digger? Nothing to mine where Daddy's finances were concerned. Whatever Louise's intent, Jolene couldn't deny her father's improved attitude.

She called Dwight.

"Jolene? Everything okay?"

"Curious if Nissie had a girl or a boy."

Fiddlers Fling

"Ted Williams Mahoney came into this world at 5:10 p.m. Mom and kid are doing fine. Jack's in seventh heaven."

"Ted Williams? Wasn't he a famous ballplayer?"

"Yep. And Jack used to play in the minors back in Chicago before he joined the Army."

A loss swept over Jolene. If things had been different, she might have been watching her own child play baseball this summer. "I'd like to get them a baby gift. Suggestions?"

"How would I know what a baby needs? I'm sure they'd appreciate anything. Money's tight right now."

She hesitated before moving on to another topic. "I'm ... embarrassed to ask, but have you noticed anything odd between my father and Louise?"

"In what way?"

"They act more like a couple than neighbors."

"Big Mike mentioned he enjoys Louise's company, but I hadn't thought it was anything romantic. Would it be so bad if they're in love?"

"If Daddy's dying, what's the point? Promise me you'll keep a close watch on Louise while I'm away."

"Fine. And while I have you on the line, any luck getting your father to sign the contracts?"

She contemplated signing them right now and bringing them over; she liked being with Dwight, even when they argued. "I have an appointment with Doc Benson tomorrow. Then I'll make up my mind if I should sign them without Daddy's co-signature or not. I'll let you know in a few days. No longer than that."

"Okay, thanks." He paused. "Umm ... on another note ... might as well jump in, though I know this sounds paranoid. Are you having me followed?"

"You're right. You're very paranoid."

"I keep running into Alicia Davenport wherever I go. I hadn't seen her in three months. Now that you're here, I see her three or four times a day. Odd places. And once, I was certain she followed me in her Lincoln Town Car."

A chill ran up Jolene's spine. So that was Alicia's car David had readied at the circle. "I don't get it. She's following me too."

Dwight laughed. "Maybe your fiancé doesn't trust me."

Or me, either. Especially around you.

Chapter Fourteen

Though the mattress was comfortable, Jolene tossed another night. She ran her fingers across her lips, reliving Dwight's kiss but remembering the sin that would forever keep them apart. She picked up the flashlight she'd brought into the room for temporary light and read from her biography of Eleanor Roosevelt.

"We must accept life as it is," Eleanor had said. She advised that mourning the past and wishing things were different held one back from making today count. Through adversity that would have devastated most people, Franklin and Eleanor brought a nation from demoralizing poverty to hope and prosperity and through a world war. Eleanor had been the voice in FDR's head. Jolene imagined she would do the same for Robert.

Her cell rang, and she checked the ID. *Robert, calling this late?* Then again, he only slept four hours a night, a driven soul much like Franklin. "Robert? What's wrong?"

"Missing you," he said. "We haven't spoken very much since you left Albany, though you promised me you'd call every day."

"Where are you?"

"New York City. I'm speaking at a union rally tomorrow. I couldn't sleep. Wish you were here. You understand unions better than I do. Frankly, I think our culture has outgrown the need for them."

Books had been written on the debate, and to open that door so late at night, more like early in the morning, seemed pointless. "We've discussed this a hundred times, Robert. It all boils down to the fact that laws in and of themselves do not protect the masses. The rich and powerful have always climbed to higher levels on the backs of the less fortunate. That's why we need advocacy groups."

"Good point. I'll use that in my speech tomorrow."

"Robert ... "

"You're upset over Alicia's hiring your father's neighbor without discussing it with you first."

"That too, as well as her inept sleuthing. She's everywhere I go except church. She's even following Dwight."

Jolene couldn't be sure, but she thought Robert made a slight growling sound. "If Alicia thinks she has to follow you and Dwight, I'm sure she has good reason. Are you two giving her cause to doubt your commitment to me?"

"Of course not. Dwight's a friend of the family. That's all."

"As for the housekeeper, I asked Alicia to arrange for her. I wanted to surprise you. I do care what happens to your father. I care about what's important to you."

"How did she know Louise was helping my father to begin with?"

"Alicia knows everything about everyone in Brookside."

"If she doesn't stop her surveillance of Dwight and me, I'm going to file a complaint. I don't think that would be good publicity for you. Did you know she's staying at the mansion? Why wasn't I told?"

"Where Alicia goes and what she does is purely her decision. Staying at our home is nothing new. Don't forget, she's a friend of the family. And yes, she sometimes operates out of the house. However, I'm not privy to her comings and goings. I'm sorry if you find her tactics annoying. She's only trying to help me, doing whatever is necessary to get you back to Albany. I need you with me."

"My father needs me more."

"Are you sure about that? Or maybe you want him to need you. He has a housekeeper, and if you signed over the business to Ashworth management, you could be home tomorrow."

Did he really miss her? Or was he manipulating her to get his hands on Murdock & Etting? "It's not that simple. I don't want to take away my father's independence. Since I've been home, he's doing much better, more energized. I'd like to see him become more engaged in the company."

"That doesn't change his diagnosis. Sooner or later, the cancer will win. You need a plan."

"That was very insensitive, Robert."

"I'm sorry. But sometimes you go a little Pollyanna on me. You need to face reality."

"I want him to feel useful, purposeful again for whatever time he has left. Is that wrong?"

"I suppose not, as long as you're not wasting your efforts, which you probably are. I heard he refused nursing services."

"Do you have spies everywhere?"

"I'm on their advisory board."

But of course. "When it comes to Brookside, what an Ashworth doesn't own, he controls ... except Murdock & Etting."

Robert quieted. "That hurt, Jolene."

"Glad to know your feelings are still capable of bruising. You've changed, Robert."

"Not really. Maybe you're the one who's changed."

"In high school, you were idealistic, critical of government reaching too far into the working man's pocketbook. Now you'd put a tax on sex."

"That's an interesting proposition. Not that it would impact me ... you've consigned me to being a monk with your puritanical views on chastity. Who does that anymore?"

"Me. Not much longer, Robert."

Anxiety filled her. She should admit her failing to Robert before their wedding night. He'd want to know who and what happened and all the gritty details she'd hoped to keep secret for eternity. If Robert knew Dwight had been her first (and only), knew she'd had an abortion, he'd be consumed with new fury against Murdock & Etting.

"Give me a few days. I'd prefer my father make his own business decisions."

"You're only delaying the inevitable, Jolene."

"I don't expect you to understand, but I'm firm on this. And as my fiancé, I want you to respect my wishes."

"You've been reading your biography of Eleanor Roosevelt again, haven't you? You're not her, and I'm not FDR, and this is not the depression."

"Goodnight, Robert." She disconnected.

Chapter Fifteen

Jolene surveyed Doc Benson's office, amused the walls were still unevenly littered with his medical degrees. Not much had changed since her last visit during the summer of her junior year at college when she had a minor cold. For most of her life, she'd enjoyed good health.

He smiled in his Marcus-Welby manner, a character familiarized through television reruns, but one who impressed her as kind and caring. Doc Benson had been the family physician for as long as Jolene could remember and delivered most of Brookside residents under the age of thirty. He must be near retirement age, but he looked the same as her childhood recollections, still sporting a full head of gray hair and a neatly trimmed goatee.

"Thank you for seeing me, Doctor Benson."

"No trouble. I watched you grow from a toothless infant to a beautiful woman. Besides, I consider your father an old and dear friend. I will always have time for you."

"I knew you and my father were boyhood friends. I need to ask, though ... did you know my mother very well? She died soon after giving birth to me, which I'm sure you know."

Doc Benson folded his hands and leaned back on his chair. "Yes, I knew your mother, and your father took her death hard. I think his responsibility to you saved him from returning to alcohol abuse. That and a strong faith, of course."

Doc Benson's secretary came in for him to sign a few papers. "Excuse me a moment, Jolene."

Fiddlers Fling

She confronted her self-recrimination—that she had waited so many years to ask about her mother. Memory pushed a little harder, to a time when she was six, curiosity prompting her to find out why she had no grandparents, aunts, or uncles like her classmates. Daddy always avoided giving her an answer. "I'll tell you when you're older, Jolene."

As a child, life never challenged her, and so she accepted her family of two as normal, assuming the mother she never knew watched from heaven. Her life was full, every moment occupied with school, music, church, beauty pageants, and exploration. She had no time for big questions, especially when the answers might bring pain. Until prom, Jolene Murdock had been the happiest child alive.

The secretary left, and Doc Benson returned his attention to Jolene. "Now, where were we? Oh yes, you asked about your mother."

"How well did you know her?"

Doc Benson's brows drooped as if he strained to scan past years, scrolling through a photo album of the mind. "Your mother moved to Brookside as a young woman. She came from Albany. Sean Ashworth's father recommended her to the school board for the position of third-grade teacher."

Was she the woman who caused the feud between Sean Ashworth and Daddy? "Did ... did my mother have any brothers or sisters? Parents?"

"Your grandmother died when your mother was a little girl. And your grandfather died before you were born."

"Do I have an uncle?"

"There was a brother, but he died in an elevator accident."

She frowned. How could she not have known about her mother's personal tragedies?

"Are you here for a biography of your mother or to talk about your father's health? You should really discuss these things with him ... soon."

"You're right. But my father never had anything good to say about the Ashworths, and now that I'm engaged to Robert, I'm trying to understand why Sean and my father despise one another so much. I'm wondering if my mother had anything to do with their feuding."

"I wouldn't call it a feud as much as lifelong animosity. Most of the current rift is political. But there are still deep personal issues at play."

"How so?"

Seemed like a simple question. Doc Benson leaned forward. "I'm not sure I'm the one who should be telling you all this, although it's Brookside history and not confidential patient information. If your father won't talk to you, you could ask your future father-in-law for his side of the story."

"There's a story?"

"I will tell you this much. Your mother was engaged to Sean Ashworth and broke the engagement to marry your father."

Doc Benson's secretary came back into the room. "You have an emergency call at the hospital."

"I'll need to respond to this, Jolene. As for your father's current condition, what do you need to know?"

She gave him a copy of the certified power of attorney she'd received from the registrar's office. "This should probably be filed in my father's medical record."

"Absolutely." He scanned the document with a handheld scanner, then typed something into his laptop. "Everything is electronic now. God help us if there's a widespread power failure and the internet goes down. I'm about ready to retire. All this high-tech medicine is getting beyond me." He tucked the paper copy into the patient file.

"Is my father really dying?"

Doc Benson lowered his gaze. "Saddens me to confirm this, but yes."

"What's his diagnosis?"

"Stage IV Liver Cancer."

Her eyes misted with the confirmation, and she harnessed the tears—no time for that. Decisions must be made. "Is there no hope? The cancer's already metastasized?"

"Chemotherapy might prolong his life but would merely be palliative, and your father has refused treatment of any kind. His right."

"Even though I have his medical power of attorney?"

Doc Benson cocked his head to one side as if he knew her question was ridiculous. "Do you really want to force your father to accept aggressive treatment that's likely to make him even sicker just to give him an extra few months?"

"Not when you put it like that."

"Besides, he signed a living will. Is he still drinking, Jolene?"

"Not since I've been home."

"That's good."

"Why didn't you call me instead of Dwight?"

"I wasn't sure how to get hold of you. Dwight said he could track you down. I probably broke a few HIPAA laws by telling him what I did, but I believed it was in your father's best interest. Sometimes a doctor has to put his patient's needs ahead of his patient's wants."

No wonder all of Brookside adored Doc Benson. She hoped he didn't retire any time soon. No one could take his place. "How long?"

"Hard to say. There are a lot of variables. If he's stopped drinking, he might have three or four months of quality life expectancy. What he needs now is good nutrition and you back in his life."

Chapter Sixteen

Jolene stopped at Phil's Bargain Furniture and picked up a small dresser and a lamp for her room before going back to the house. She found a note on the table.

Gone shopping with Louise.

She should be glad Daddy's neighbor managed to get him away from the television and out of the house. Why stay any longer? Why bother to fix up a room she didn't truly need?

Perhaps she should sign the papers for Dwight and go back to Albany tomorrow. She dragged the dresser upstairs and placed it near her bed. Should she bother to put any clothes in it if she were leaving so soon? Her head swam after talking with Doc Benson and learning facts she'd never known. Her father was no longer the giant of a man she defied. He'd lost a wife, yet put his grief aside to raise an ungrateful daughter.

Most adolescents, she reasoned, were self-centered, giving little thought to their parents except as people who provided shelter, food, and unconditional love—a love she tested time and time again. Her teenage years, until prom, had been uncomplicated, each day filled with goodness. No need for questions then.

Deep in memory, she barely noticed her iPhone creeping across her bed. She had muted it while at Doc Benson's and had yet to reset her ringtone. She checked the number. *Mother Mary.*

"This is Jolene."

"When are you coming back, dear?"

"I'm fine. How are you?"

"Yes, that was rather abrupt, wasn't it? I assume you're doing well, since you spoke with Robert only last night. He's rather miffed."

Too bad, Robert. "I appreciate your concern, but Robert and I are grownups. We can handle our own arguments. All couples have them, don't they?" Or maybe Sean and Mother Mary saw each other so seldom they didn't fight. He had his own bedroom suite at the Albany estate.

From time to time, the question arose in Jolene's mind why Mary Ashworth had approved, even encouraged, her son's engagement to a commoner when history recorded the Ashworths consistently married into big money. Royalty always sought out royalty for their offspring. The question that followed was equally troubling. If men married women like their mothers, in what ways did Jolene Murdock resemble Mary Ashworth?

"You know I don't like to interfere ..."

Jolene turned her mouth away from the phone and covered her smirk.

"But this is a very critical time for Robert's campaign. Voters have always warmed to you, Jolene. You are Robert's biggest asset."

An asset? What happened to love? Why must she be the one required to make the sacrifices? Wasn't marriage supposed to be give and take?

Is that what happened to Eleanor and Franklin? Had she realized she was less of a wife and more of an asset? Though she gave him everything, he'd turned his affection toward Lucy Mercer.

"Politics do little to thrill me. I embrace the process because I love *him*, not the game."

"Then you know how important this campaign is to him. If you love—"

"That's not fair. My being here with my father has nothing to do with whether I love Robert or not. I shouldn't have to choose between them."

"No one expects that of you, dear. I can't help wondering, though, if perhaps you don't want to come back."

Did she?

"I'm looking forward to the wedding and being Robert's wife. Sometimes life requires us to put our most treasured plans on hold for a greater purpose. I don't expect you to understand."

"I do, more than you realize, dear. I had a father."

"Of course, you did."

"I adored him. He died when I was only sixteen—cancer. I bargained with God and told Him if he'd let my father live, I'd serve him to my dying day. My prayers fell on deaf ears."

For the past three years, she'd seen Mother Mary as an austere, unfeeling woman—a woman so cold the air dipped ten degrees when she entered a room. Yet, Jolene still craved the woman's opinion and approval. Dread drenched like a tropical rainfall. Would she become a casualty like Mary Ashworth, more concerned about appearances than actually living life?

Jolene sighed. She couldn't fight both Robert and his mother. And of the two, Mother Mary had the more dominant personality, a powerful pull that sucked Jolene's will dry. "If you must know, I plan on coming back to Albany tomorrow after I talk with my father's attorney." Determination rose. *Family is family*. "But of this much you can be certain. No matter what, I won't put Ashworth interests over Murdock & Etting."

"You don't plan on running the company while on the campaign trail, do you?"

"No. The logical solution is to make Dwight Etting CEO."

"Humph. Really?"

"Yes. I told Robert I'll need to make frequent visits to Brookside to monitor my father's illness. Alicia will find a way to put a positive spin on his situation."

"Of course, dear, but you're acting emotionally rather than from practicality. I'm not sure Dwight Etting can be trusted."

"Why not?"

"He did father a child with you ... one you aborted. Did he not?"

That she'd ever confided in Mary Ashworth topped the list of Jolene's regrets. She disconnected.

Chapter Seventeen

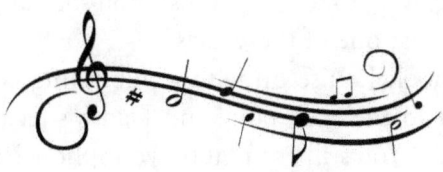

Her cell vibrated as it played "Orange Blossom Special." This time Jolene let Mother Mary's call go to voice mail. Probably a scold for being so rude and a lecture on the proper way to end an uncomfortable conversation. Cutting her off so abruptly would probably stir more accusations. *So be it. The woman crossed a line.* Nor could Jolene bear reliving her worst mistake with someone as frigid as Mary Ashworth. That the woman Jolene most despised was the one to whom she owed the most had to be the ultimate irony. Jolene glanced at her watch. Near one o'clock. Hopefully her father and Louise had returned, and Louise had gone home, giving Jolene a chance to talk to Daddy without the neighbor hanging on every word, injecting her own opinions. Seemed she stayed at the house like a kitchen fixture, plugged in and ready to serve.

Jolene went downstairs. They sat at the kitchen table, acting like an old married couple—Louise knitting while Daddy read the paper. Louise greeted Jolene with a motherly smile. Did the woman have to be so pleasant?

"Thought your father might enjoy some homemade soup."

"He always liked when I made soup for him. What kind is it?"

"Beef and barley. Hot and full of vegetables."

Daddy laughed. "Women always find a way to push vegetables on us meat-and-potatoes men. Good soup, Jolene. Have some." He dunked a slice of homemade bread into the broth.

How much he'd improved, in many ways resembling his old self. Even his attire—khakis and a flannel shirt—had always been Daddy's daily preference except for church. Then he'd put on a sports jacket and a tie. She'd thought him handsome, for a father. He'd trim his beard, splash a little cologne, and slick his hair back with a dab of men's styling cream. The single women of the church flocked for his attention, some bringing him pastries or a casserole. On the way home, he'd wink and say, "These women are good cooks, but not as good as my Jolene." She wanted him to tell her Louise's cooking wasn't as good as his little girl's. Was that wrong?

Jolene ladled a bowl of Louise's soup, careful to give her the adulation the woman seemed to crave. "Excellent, Louise. You should write a cookbook."

"Might just do that one of these days."

She'd offer to hook Louise up with a publishing company owned by the Ashworths, but Jolene's cell rang, and Daddy's feet tapped in rhythm to her signature hail. "You still got that on your phone? I thought you gave up country."

"I like the song, even if I don't play my fiddle anymore."

She checked the ID, grateful it wasn't Mother Mary. "Dwight?"

"Just wanted you to know we'll finish up the attic stairs tomorrow morning. How's Big Mike today?"

"Ask him yourself." Jolene handed the phone over. "It's Dwight. Wants to know how you are today."

Daddy scowled, and Louise laughed. "Talk, Michael. Dwight's a good boy."

"Never liked talking on these things. Guess I'm older than my years in a lot of ways." He put the phone near his mouth and shouted into it. "Doing fine, Dwight. How about yourself?" Hesitation ... then, "Louise made some soup. Had your lunch yet?"

He gave the cell back to Jolene.

"What did Dwight say?"

"Coming over in a bit."

Louise smiled. "I'll be sure to keep the soup hot for him. Jolene, how's the room coming along?"

"It would be nice to put up a few pictures or find a desk or shelf of some kind. Anything in the attic?"

Daddy tilted his head back and gazed at the ceiling as if the answer to her question was written above. "Don't remember for sure. I ain't stepped foot up there in ages."

He hadn't said "Since you left," but she felt the sting in his words. Her heart constricted, and she found herself speaking aloud rather than weighing her words and biting her tongue. "Oh, Daddy, I'm so sorry I hurt you. Please try to understand I love Robert. I want to be a good wife. Not just that, but as his wife, I can do a lot of good for Brookside."

Louise shot Daddy a glance, and he moved his lips as if to say something, then took another piece of bread and slathered it with butter.

He took a bite, chewing like a man who has no dentures—only he still had all his teeth.

She'd poured out her heart, and he chose to ignore her, his silence more painful than outright condemnation.

He glanced at her, eyes strangely sparkling, like they used to before he sent her on an Easter Scavenger Hunt. "Might be some pictures up there."

Louise stood. "Want me to scope it out for you, Jolene? I'm sure you got other things to do than hunt in that crammed attic."

Daddy winked and motioned for Louise to sit. "Check the back corner, Jolene. Seems I remember stuffing a few things there." He took another bite of bread.

"I'll do that."

Closing the door behind her, she climbed the attic steps. The stairs squeaked, but the banister Dwight's crew built made her feel more secure. When she reached the landing, she stubbed her toe against a rectangular metal box. She flipped the light switch, then opened her father's favorite chest, a one-drawer Stanley toolbox with an array of compartments filled with screws and nails. It had once belonged to her grandfather and had then been used by Daddy. At the end of every workday, he left it near the back door. That he'd chosen to tuck it away in the attic told Jolene that Big Mike Murdock had no intention of returning to work.

She zigzagged through the few open spaces—mountains of piled boxes and totes cluttered the floor everywhere she looked. A shadow caught her attention, and she fought her way toward the back, rearranging the plethora of stored memorabilia along the way. She opened some of the totes, gasping when she found her mother's china, precariously placed upon odd-shaped boxes, but heartened her father hadn't sold the collection. She moved the precious tote to a more secure position, hoping to take them back to Albany, if permitted. She resumed her quest to explore the reaches of Daddy's attic wonderland.

Fiddlers Fling

The closer she came to the shadow, the more it took form—something wrapped in a tarp, set upon a tower of boxes blocked by stacks of old lumber and bricks. She noticed writing on the outside of the bins, but there wasn't enough light to read the scribbled information. She went back to the toolbox and found a flashlight, then repositioned the lumber and bricks to the other side of the attic. Finally able to get to the tower, she shone the light on the boxes. She gasped as she read the labels. *Jolene's Room.*

Her heart skipped several beats, heartened that Daddy hadn't discarded her memories, merely stored them where perhaps someday she'd find them. She couldn't open any of the boxes without taking down the wrapped object at the top. She circled the attic again, looking for a step stool or something she could climb. Finding an old oak chair sturdy enough to stand on, she dragged it to where her past was stored. She took down the object. Carefully removing the tarp, she squeaked with astonishment—her fiddle!

More amazing than the rediscovery of her childhood, Daddy had *led* her to them. She nested the fiddle under her chin and slid the bow back and forth, tuning the instrument as best she could under these conditions. She plucked a few strings.

Somewhere in her memory, the hymn came to life. And she sweetly played the tune from so many years ago, singing the words in her heart: "Amazing Grace, how sweet the sound ... "

They'd first played the duet when Jolene was only five. Visions of those precious times tripped in her mind, flicking before her, an album of their once unbreakable bond. What happened to that little girl? As she began the second stanza, soft alto tones came from behind her as if vivid recall jarred auditory hallucinations. She turned to see Daddy's bow sliding tremulously over his fiddle, his eyes moistened with a father's love. This hunt had been designed, his quiet way of offering forgiveness. She ran into his arms while a confused Louise looked on.

Chapter Eighteen

Louise slapped the bannister. "That's the prettiest music I've heard in years. I didn't know either one of you played an instrument."

Daddy squeezed Jolene's hand. "Stopped playing a long time ago."

Jolene put her head on Daddy's shoulder. "So did I."

Louise clucked. "Well, now, I call that a downright shame. Any particular reason you two gave up? You're both so good."

Daddy glanced toward Jolene, his eyes deep with sorrow. "No particular reason."

Jolene's head drooped. "My fiancé dislikes fiddle music. He prefers the violin."

Louise's chuckle bounced from the rafters. "I hear the only difference between a fiddle and violin is the kind of music folks play on it. What I just heard could've been a violin for sure. It was that beautiful."

A voice from downstairs called up. "Where is everybody? Soup's on the stove, but I don't see anyone."

Louise leaned over the landing. "We're up here, Dwight. Jolene and Michael are about to give us a concert."

Dwight made his way into the attic, glancing back and forth from Big Mike to Jolene. "What's going on?"

Fiddlers Fling

Louise leaned against the bannister as she stroked her chin. "I think we ought to bring these fiddles downstairs and see what these two can do. Sound good to you, Dwight?"

Dwight could tell something spiritual, even life-changing had happened in this attic apart from his witness. He shot up thanks, just to see Jolene and Big Mike holding their fiddles at the same time and in the same room. "Sounds great to me, Louise."

Big Mike took a rag and dusted off his fiddle. "What do you say, Jolene? Want to have a jam session?"

Jolene looked at Dwight. "We'd be missing a keyboard."

Big Mike smiled. "You and I can warm up while Dwight gets it."

Coincidence or God's impeccable timing? "Actually, it's in the truck. I planned on going over to the church from here to set up for prayer meeting tonight."

Big Mike took a step toward the landing. "Why you standing there, boy? Bring it in."

Jolene's pleading look cemented Dwight's decision. He was supposed to practice with the worship band in an hour. He'd call Pastor Tim and let him know the Lord had a different rehearsal in mind.

Dwight had set up the keyboard in record time, slurping down a bowl of Louise's soup in the process. He strained to remember the last time there had been a jam session in Big Mike's living room. Probably for the Christmas concert at the church during his senior year.

His father had written that Jolene and Big Mike continued to play during Jolene's summer vacations from college. Dwight caught the last concert while on leave between his first and second tours in Afghanistan. Jolene had played mechanically as if merely going through the steps for Big Mike's sake.

Louise sat in an armchair and clapped in anticipation, then darted back up, grabbed her purse, and took out her smartphone. "Need to get a picture of this!" She snapped while the trio posed then she returned to her chair.

Everyone looked ready, and Dwight nodded to Big Mike and Jolene. "What would you like to play?"

Without hesitation, Big Mike blurted out, "Devil Went Down to Georgia."

Dwight liked the song, but even as a kid he was frustrated that Big Mike's band often played songs popular when their grandparents were kids. Yet, he loved the challenge of the old standbys. This particular song jived with soul, telling how a man can be twisted and pulled by the devil's wiles, yet God always triumphed.

Neither Jolene nor her father had played in recent years. When they'd performed it in the past, Dwight had taken the vocals. "Don't know if I remember the words."

Big Mike laughed. "I'm the one with the cancer brain, Dwight. If I can remember, you sure should. Jolene, you be Johnny's fiddle and I'll play the devil's. Take the bridge too."

As Dwight sang the lyrics, he thought how much Jolene struggled for her soul. *Help her, Lord.* The chords gushed from his memory onto his keyboard, and Dwight ripped an introduction. Big Mike and Jolene kept up with no difficulty, a few mistakes here and there, only noticeable when Jolene scrunched her brows together as if announcing her misfire.

The song ended to Louise's standing ovation, cheers, whistles, and claps. "Well, I'll be dipped, Michael. Shame you don't play more."

Big Mike sat on the sofa, breathing heavily as if winded.

Jolene cast a worried glance. "Too much, Daddy?"

"Not at all. Just ain't used to the exertion. I'd forgotten how much energy a song like that takes."

Jolene rested her fiddle against the wall. "Thank you, Dwight. We don't want to hold you up any longer from your church responsibility."

"If you'd like to keep playing, I'm sure the church can hold a prayer meeting without me."

Resting her fiddle, she exhaled, stretched out her hands and then rolled her head. "I agree with Daddy. That was a workout. We can play more if Daddy wants to."

Big Mike nodded. "Sure would. But give me a minute or two to recuperate."

"Dwight, since you're staying, would you go for a quick walk with me?"

"Sure."

"We won't be long, Daddy. Rest up because Dwight will probably pick out another rouser."

"I'd like that, little girl."

Chapter Nineteen

Dwight opened the back door, signaling Jolene to exit first. "Where to?"

"Let's take the road—easier walking. The music made me a little winded too. Felt good, though."

The sun burst on Dwight's rejuvenated hopes, as Jolene struggled to keep up with his long strides. "You haven't lost your touch, Jolene. You're still better than all of them. Big Mike's a little shaky, but he remembers every nuance of the song. Kept up pretty good too."

"He surprised me as well. I wish I could play with him again before—"

"Don't say it, Jolene. I know it pains you. I have an idea, though."

"What?"

"The annual Fiddlers Fling is in a few weeks."

She stopped cold. "You can't possibly think we'd be in any shape to compete that soon! And I need to get back to Albany. I have a wedding coming up in a month. Remember?"

He'd sooner forget and would if Jolene didn't remind him at every turn. Incredulous after all they shared that she still wanted to marry that creep. "Let me ask you something, Jolene."

"Ask. I won't promise to answer."

"Do you love Robert? I mean, really love him?"

She looked into his eyes. "What do you mean by that?"

"You know."

"No, I don't."

Fiddlers Fling

He lifted her chin. "Like we used to be in love?"

She removed his hand and turned away. "We were kids. Puppy love."

"I think it was a lot more than that, Jolene. I have to say this ... regardless of what you decide about Robert. I still love you. I always will."

"You're in love with a memory, Dwight. I'm not that girl anymore."

"And I'm not that boy. Yes, I know. We've changed, matured, however you want to describe it. Yet, we're still the same people. You playing the fiddle just now proved it. Promise me one thing—if you marry Robert Ashworth, you won't give up the real you. She's come alive again in the few days you've been here. I'd hate to see her buried in an Ashworth version of a wife's decorum."

"You think that's all I am to Robert? A trophy wife? You can't presume to know his feelings for me."

"Maybe not. But when a man loves a woman for who she truly is, he supports her talents, doesn't make her give them up. Besides, you're avoiding my question. Do you love Robert?"

"Yes, I love Robert. No, not the same way I love you—"

Dwight grabbed her arm and spun her around to face him. "You said, 'love,' not 'loved,' as in past tense."

She removed his hand from her arm. "Slip of the tongue."

He kissed her, and she returned the passion, abruptly shoving him away. "Fine. I admit it. I do love you, Dwight. But we cannot happen. Whatever we had ended a long time ago."

"Why? You felt the chemistry while we played. I know you did."

"Too much has happened."

"Like what?"

"Life. I can't talk about this, Dwight. I'm going to marry Robert. That's final."

Everything in his being wanted to pull her back into his world.

Wait.

He caught his breath. *For what, Lord?*

There is much you do not know.

"All right," he conceded. "If I can't stop you, don't expect me to cheer as you throw your life away."

Jolene resumed walking, her face taut with determination. Dwight followed. "I didn't ask you to walk with me so you could make me feel like a fool."

"That was not my intention, and you know it. So why are we walking?"

"I have an appointment with Gordon Brockway, Jr., tomorrow. I want you there."

"Why?"

"Daddy essentially has given me permission to make whatever decisions I think are best for Murdock & Etting. Although I believe he only said that because he's given up caring. Robert wants me to assign management to Ashworth Enterprises. I won't do that. Not as long as it's possible to keep the business afloat. Would you be willing to act as CEO?"

"Any chance your father would agree to talk to the attorney with us?"

"I'll ask. Assuming he agrees to the arrangement, are you willing?"

"Anything for Big Mike ... and you. How will this arrangement, as you call it, set with your future in-laws?"

"On this one matter, I stand firm. I told Mother Mary as much. I will *not* sign the business over to the Ashworths ... ever. You have my word, even if that means I have to put a prenup into our wedding agreement."

How he wanted to embrace her, to wrap her as a parent subdues a child in the throes of a temper tantrum. Yet Dwight knew that without the why, he must let Jolene flounder and let God do the rescuing.

Chapter Twenty

Jolene eyed the photograph of Gordon Brockway, Jr., his wife, and their two little boys. Brockway's old office must have had a recent overhaul. She vaguely remembered Gordon's son who graduated two years ahead of Robert. The older Brockway's rooms sported minty-colored walls and shag carpet;—young Gordon had repainted in a vibrant scarlet, laid down mauve carpet, placed greens in every corner, and hung Monet posters in the waiting areas and office spaces.

"How's Robert these days?" Gordon asked. "I knew he went to Harvard after we graduated, but until I saw his campaign notice, I wasn't sure what had happened to him. He and I didn't travel in the same circles."

"Rumor has it you've always beaten your own drum." Jolene smiled, reason enough to like Gordon, Jr., besides the fact he had no political ambition for himself and was anxious to see new business come into Brookside.

Daddy shook Gordon's hand. "Nice to see you, young man. I hear you're doing good things as the new party chair. Keep it up."

Gordon eyed Jolene. "Can't believe you're actually engaged to an Ashworth. I'm not surprised. Ashworth men like beautiful women."

Her cheeks heated, and Dwight leaned forward. "About Murdock & Etting."

Gordon tapped the file on his desk, then reread Jolene's power of attorney document. "Jolene, I agree with your plan. Mr. Murdock? How do you feel about these arrangements?"

Fiddlers Fling

"I'd prefer Jolene run the company, but she has another life to get on with. I trust Dwight."

Gordon secured the required signatures, signed as notary, and shook hands with everyone concerned. "All set."

Robert would be livid, and Mary Ashworth would likely flood Jolene's in-box as to why making Dwight CEO showed poor judgment on Jolene's part. She hitched her faux-leather purse over her shoulder. As they left the building, Daddy, eyes begging like a dog's for a bone, pulled Dwight to the side. "Up for another jam session before Jolene has to leave?"

"Sure. What about you, Jolene?"

"Absolutely." One last chance to play her fiddle—or maybe she'd bring it back to Albany with her and play when Ashworth eyes were elsewhere.

Dwight tugged his cap. "I have to go to the office, make arrangements to start on the new contracts, and hire back as many of the men as possible. Is four too late?"

"I can stay a couple of extra hours, I guess." How she'd like to stay forever! But life required her to ride the train away from fiddles and building contracts. "Daddy, would you wait for me in the car?"

"Hurry it up. Louise has lunch waiting."

"Walk with me, Dwight."

He helped her down the stairs. When she returned to Albany, she'd shed designer ladders for pumps. Not every senator's wife wore Jimmy Choos. "You're still going back this evening?"

"Louise wants to take care of Daddy. The business will be up and running again. I'd say my work here is done."

Dwight scowled. "Far from it, but I see your mind's made up. What about the fling?"

"About that. Maybe you could help my father enter. Play the keyboard for him?"

"Won't be the same without you."

"I think playing the fiddle again would be good therapy for Daddy."

"Of course, I'll jam with him. Mahoney would come too. You don't have to ask, Jolene."

They turned to walk back. As they neared the house, she spotted Daddy sprawled on the sidewalk, flailing like an overturned turtle. "Daddy!" She rushed to his side. "Are you hurt?"

"Got a little dizzy and fell."

Jolene felt his pulse ... erratic. His eyes darted back and forth, then started to roll back. "Daddy, stay with us! You can't leave me now. You hear me? Dwight, call an ambulance!"

Jolene rode in the ambulance with her father, and Dwight followed in his truck. Daddy seemed more responsive. "We'll be at the hospital soon, Daddy. Stay awake."

"Sing to me."

"What do you want to hear?"

"Whispering Hope."

"That's a real old song. I'm not sure I remember it."

"Your mother and I used to sing it."

"Daddy, tell me about my mother."

"She was beautiful. Sang like an angel. You look just like her."

"How did you meet?"

"Sean Ashworth introduced us. I built cabinets on his father's estate. She'd come to the mansion to visit Sean."

"How did my mother know Sean?"

"Well, now, that's a funny story. See, Sean and your mother were engaged. But I took one look at your mother, and I knew she didn't belong to somebody as cold as an Ashworth."

His eyelids fluttered.

"No, Daddy! Stay awake. Tell me more."

He took deep breaths and moaned before continuing. "I asked her to help me study for my GED. Hadn't thought I wanted to get it after I dropped out of school, but I figured it was a way of seeing more of your mother."

Jolene laughed. "Why, you sly fox, you."

He smiled. "I took lessons at her apartment, and sometimes we took the lessons to the river. She taught me history and hollered when I didn't use good grammar. I knew better, but it got her so agitated, I slipped a few *ain'ts* and verb disagreements just to see the look on her face. I still don't speak the Queen's English very good." He gazed upward. "I figure she's stomping a foot at me from heaven right now."

"I always knew you were a smart man."

Fiddlers Fling

"Your mother taught me Shakespeare, and I taught her how to skip pebbles on the water." He grabbed Jolene's hand. "Feeling kinda faint, little girl."

The ambulance reached the hospital, and staff brought her father into the emergency room. Jolene waited in the lobby, glad when Dwight arrived. He held her hand, and this time she didn't pull away.

They sat together, neither one speaking. She sensed his worry for her father equaled her own. Finally Doc Benson came to the waiting room.

"Your father's going to be okay ... well, at least from the fall. He's got quite a goose egg. I'm keeping him overnight for observation. He may have had a slight concussion, but the CAT scan is negative. If all's well, he can go home tomorrow. He'll need someone to look after him twenty-four-seven for a few days."

Jolene nodded and Doc Benson left the lounge.

"Will you give me a ride to my car? I'd like to pick it up while they're getting my father settled. No need for you to stay any longer."

"No problem. I take it you're not leaving tonight."

"I'll stay until I know Daddy's all right and to make sure Louise can take on the extra duty."

"Extra duty for what?" Louise rounded the corner just as Jolene and Dwight exited the waiting room.

"Louise, how did you know we were here?"

"I have a scanner in my den ... heard the 911 call. I figured it was Michael from the location, age, and symptoms. Got here as quick as I could. How is he?"

"He gave us a scare, but it looks like nothing more than a bump on the head. He'll come home tomorrow, but he'll need more care. We'll pay extra."

"Mind if we go back into the lounge a minute?"

They sat back down in the waiting area, Louise's expression an enigma. "I've been meaning to talk to you about my caring for Michael."

Please don't tell me you want to quit. "He really likes having you around."

"I got a confession to make."

"Anything to do with Nursing Services?"

"Some. See, I quit because one of the patients said I stole money. No one believed the patient, but I didn't need the money or the aggravation. Thing is, I really do like your father, Jolene."

"Then what's the problem?"

"It's that Alicia woman who hired me the day you came. The next day I saw her go into the house, and I knew Michael was napping. I got suspicious, so I checked up on her—looked through the window. I saw her take Michael's checkbook out of the drawer and stick it up in the high cupboard. She took his newspaper too. When she came off the stool, she noticed me. Opened the door and yanked me inside. Said if I told anyone she'd report me to the police for stealing. Now, why does she want to go and do a thing like that for? I don't want people accusing me of being dishonest, but I can't abide anyone being mean to Michael. I'll still look after your father, but I won't take no money for it."

Jolene stiffened. "My father will insist on paying you. Please don't quit. I'll straighten this out with Miss Davenport. If my father trusts you, that's good enough for me."

"Call me when Michael gets out of the hospital, and I'll come right over with some eats. I left the chicken potpie in the fridge, so help yourselves when you get back to the house. Okay if I go see Michael now?"

"Certainly."

Louise left, and Jolene laughed at the ludicrousness of it all.

Dwight cocked his head to one side. "What's so funny?"

"Guess I won't be going back to Albany for a bit longer. Going to get into a hen fight tomorrow."

Chapter Twenty-one

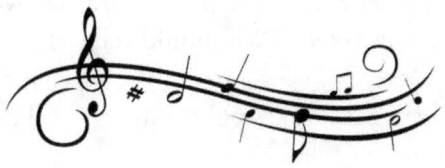

The afternoon sun sent fractured beams through the dirty windows, its generated heat was suffocating. Jolene opened the den patio door to let fresh air in while she polished her fiddle, determined more than ever to bring it with her when she returned to Albany.

She mused over the conversation with Dwight the night before, having called him from Daddy's hospital room. "My father needs one last fling," she'd nearly pleaded. "He said he wouldn't sign up unless I played too. I can't disappoint him, so I'm staying a little longer."

"That's great, Jolene," Dwight had said.

And at lunch, Daddy had seemed as pleased as Dwight when she told him the news while he gobbled a grilled cheese sandwich Louise had made when they came home from the hospital.

His spirits animated whenever Louise was near, and Jolene was glad she'd invited Louise to tag along to the hospital to bring Daddy home. Jolene snickered as she recalled the ride home from the hospital. She'd made a quick stop at the IGA store to purchase a supply of low-calorie frozen dinners. Louise scowled when Jolene flung the bag of groceries into the car, a dinner entree sticking out at the top.

"Your cooking is wonderful, Louise, but please understand. I have a wedding dress to fit into when I get back. Daddy needs the calories—I don't."

Fiddlers Fling

As soon as they arrived home, Louise set about the kitchen to prepare lunch and gathered the ingredients for chocolate cake. Jolene sighed. More temptation.

Dwight's call brought her back to the present. "We're all signed up for the fling. I'm really glad you changed your mind."

"I think my mind got changed for me."

Jolene walked into the kitchen. "Daddy, Dwight says he's signed us up for the fling."

Her father's smile made the anticipated extra stay worth the while. He looked hopeful when he asked, "We should rehearse this afternoon, don't you think?"

"You're probably right." She spoke into the cell. "Daddy wants to rehearse this afternoon."

"I only have to make one stop at a job site. Mahoney said he'd help out."

"Shouldn't he be home with his brand new baby?"

"Probably looking for an excuse to get out of the house."

"Daddy, Dwight says Jack Mahoney's going to join our group."

"Jack plays almost as mean a guitar as you do the fiddle, little girl."

"Okay on the rehearsal, but make it later. I have to see Alicia."

Daddy and Louise stared, and Dwight snorted. "You aren't really going to beat her up, are you?"

"I haven't decided yet."

"That's a fight I'd pay top-dollar to watch."

"I'm sure you would."

"There's a fundraiser Sunday afternoon at the Adult Center. It would be a good warm up for the contest. What do you think?"

"Hold on for a minute." Jolene switched the cell to speaker and laid it on the kitchen table. "There, that's better. Now we're all on the same page."

Daddy glared at the phone. "If you ask me, sounds more like we're reading different books."

"Do you want to play at the benefit?" Dwight asked.

Daddy nodded. "Sure. In for a penny, in for a pound, as they say."

Jolene snickered. "With Louise's cooking, I'm in for several pounds."

Louise clucked disproval. "You're too skinny, Jolene. Ain't nothing to let out a dress. Those frozen dinners wouldn't keep a maggot alive. They're too smart to eat 'em."

Dwight's chuckle lifted Jolene's mood, his enjoyment for life an elixir for her troubled spirit. She'd miss him terribly when she returned to Albany. "I take it your wonderful fiancé is not thrilled with your decision to stay longer."

"I imagine not."

"You haven't spoken to him?"

"I texted him last night to let him know my father had fallen, and the doctor thought I shouldn't leave for a few days. Robert's tried to call several times and so has his mother, but I really don't want to talk to either one of them right now."

"Forever the rebel, I see."

A loud knock on the door shook the house. "I'll be back in a sec. Someone's at the door."

Daddy looked up. "Never mind the door, little girl. Sit and eat. Let Louise get it. She's good at shooing away unwanted company."

Jolene headed toward the living room. "I promise I'll eat in a minute. You and Dwight talk about the benefit until I get back. I'd like a little more information."

She didn't want to say who she suspected ... four staccato raps, loud and decisive. This time she had no excuse. She opened the door. Three days ago, she'd have fallen into his arms. For the first time, she realized the resemblance to his father, all six-foot-two of him—his sandy blond hair cut slightly longer than military, broad shoulders and a narrow waist that in a Speedo made every girl's head turn. His rigid stance spelled ire, his hazel eyes wild with fury, his face crimson. She braced herself for the coming lecture. "Robert, what are you doing here?"

"To bring you to Albany and back to your senses."

"Daddy's fine. Thanks for asking."

He stepped into the living room.

"We were having lunch. Have you eaten? Louise made a wonderful potpie, and there're leftovers in the fridge." Not waiting for his refusal, Jolene walked to the kitchen, Robert trailing behind, his clip agitated, like that of an unruly child being dragged from a store. Maybe once he saw how much her father had improved, he'd understand her need to stay longer, to enjoy these good moments while they lasted. Kindness was not Robert's strength, but logic sometimes helped him see the benefit of compassion.

Fiddlers Fling

Louise and Daddy looked up as they entered the kitchen, and Robert's rigid posture relaxed for his audience. "Mr. Murdock, I apologize for the interruption, but you know as well as I do how stubborn your daughter is."

Daddy shrugged his shoulders, pressed his lips together, and said nothing.

Robert glanced toward Louise. "You must be Mr. Murdock's housekeeper." He offered her a politician's handshake, and Louise reluctantly accepted. "Robert Ashworth. I hope I can count on your vote in November."

"I ain't decided yet." She took the potpie out of the refrigerator and grabbed another plate from the cupboard. "Now, sit yourself down, Mr. Ashworth. Jolene can wait until after lunch to leave. Won't have all that food going to waste."

Robert glared at Louise's casserole. "My parents expected to meet us after I picked up Jolene."

Must he always be so presumptuous? "And you couldn't let me know ahead of time?"

"If you'd bother to listen to your voice mail, you'd have known we were coming."

Amusement splattered on Daddy's face. "Sean Ashworth actually set foot in Brookside? Don't tell me hell finally froze over."

Robert glanced at Jolene. "I see where your gift of sarcasm comes from."

She planted firm feet but gripped the table for added determination. "I'm not going anywhere. Give my apologies to your parents. I think I'll enjoy Louise's wonderful food instead." She plopped down in a chair in front of the plate Louise had prepared for Robert, took a fork and dug in. "This is really delicious. Robert, you don't know what you're missing."

He leaned over Jolene's right shoulder and turned her head toward him, the red in his cheeks deepening. "I need you to leave with me right now."

"I'm not going anywhere." She turned away and took another bite.

Robert straightened his tie. "Is this because of what Louise said Alicia did? I'm sure it was all a misunderstanding—one I promise to straighten out after we meet my parents."

Daddy looked at Louise. "What misunderstanding?"

Louise crossed her arms. "Miss Davenport wanted to make it look like you were losing your mind. She moved your checkbook."

"That so, Ashworth?" Daddy said. "Sounds like something your father would do. Didn't expect it from a pretty lady like Miss Davenport. Mind telling me why she—or you, for that matter—wanted Jolene to think ... Oh, I see. You hoped Jolene would put me in a nursing home and let you run things."

"Mr. Murdock, you shouldn't be living alone."

"I'm not alone. I got Jolene, Louise, and Dwight. I ain't going to no nursing home. That's final."

"You forget Jolene has your power of attorney. She could decide that for you."

Daddy stood. "Is that right, Jolene? You'd make me go against my wishes?"

"No."

Robert picked up Jolene's fiddle off the counter. "What's this?"

Daddy laughed. "It's a fiddle, Mr. Harvard."

"I'm not blind. I know it's a fiddle. Is this yours, Jolene?"

"We're practicing."

"For what?"

"Apparently you know my moves almost before I do. You tell me."

"Fine. Yes, I know about the Fiddlers Fling, and I absolutely forbid it." Robert's knowledge, so quickly after the fact, left one logical conclusion. He'd been monitoring her calls. This time Robert had gone too far.

Before she could give voice to her feelings, he continued. "It's not just about the wedding. I need you by my side. I have three major campaign events coming up. Your absence is raising too many questions."

Jolene stood and met Robert's glare. "I think you should leave."

His expression turned blank. "Oh, I'm leaving. But not without you. No fiancée of mine is going to take part in a country hoedown. I won't have it."

Jolene grabbed her fiddle from Robert, one last stand against his unreasonableness. "First of all, you don't own me. Second, you're my fiancé, not God. And third, I'll play in that contest if I so choose. If you can't 'have' it, this engagement is off."

He pulled at her arm. "Jolene, you're being entirely unreasonable."

Daddy rose and slammed a fist on the table. "You heard Jolene. Either leave now, or I'm calling the police and suing you for harassment. I won't tolerate anyone manhandling my daughter, especially in her own house."

Fiddlers Fling

Jolene willed her knees to stop wobbling. What had she done? Put her engagement in jeopardy for the sake of a country contest? No, there was something much more important at stake. She must take her stand or be forever ruled by Robert's will. As his wife, she'd of course support him in his political interests, but she refused to give up her right to independent thought. Eleanor became her own person and followed her own agenda, especially when her personal integrity differed from that of Franklin. She changed the world without becoming his pillow. "Well, Robert? Do I give you back your ring?"

He tugged at his burgundy blazer. "Tell me it's a one-time thing, and I'll overlook this craziness. Alicia will find a way to spin the contest to gain voter appeal. It's what she's good at."

Jolene froze.

"It *is* a one-time thing, isn't it?"

"So what if it's not? What if I miss playing my fiddle and want to take playing back up? Music is a part of me, and I expect the man I marry to support that, not deprive me of it."

Without a word, Robert left, slamming the door behind him.

The light flickered on her cell, and she picked it up, switching off speaker mode. "I didn't know you were still on the line. I'm sorry you had to listen to all that."

"I can't believe you're still willing to marry that jerk after the way he acted."

"That's my decision to make."

"Mahoney and I will be at the house by four."

"See you later." She disconnected.

Daddy sat back down. "I agree with Dwight. Why do you insist on marrying that son of a—"

"Daddy!"

"Just calling it like I see it."

"Robert can try to be controlling sometimes, but I can handle him."

"That's what your mother tried to tell me when she was engaged to young Ashworth's father."

Jolene sat. "Now there's a story I have to hear."

"Alright ... but only to prove my point. Babs—that's my nickname for your mother—we'd take lots of walks by the river, and we fell in love. She finally saw that marrying an Ashworth wouldn't be right. I suggested we run off and elope, but she said she owed it to Sean to break it off face to face."

"Is that why Sean despises you so much?"

"More to it than that, little girl. Sean must have sensed there was something between Babs and me. He followed us that day and must've heard what Babs said. When he saw us kissing, he jumped out from hiding and punched me in the nose, then pushed me into the river. He was thin, but he was strong. Got his hands around my throat and tried to drown me."

Jolene felt the blood drain from her head. "Sean Ashworth is a ruthless man, I'll admit," she croaked, her throat constricted. "But ... murder?"

"I wasn't born into privilege like Sean, and folks like him looked down on us farm boys. But I never had murder in my heart for anyone like Sean Ashworth did for me that day. He'd of killed me for sure if Babs hadn't taken a fallen branch and hit him hard enough to knock him off his feet. She threw her engagement ring at him and we took off, and he kept shouting he'd get even. We got married a week later."

Jolene laughed. "I imagine Sean tells a different version."

"More'n likely. Couldn't have been that brokenhearted, though. He got engaged to Mary shortly after. 'Course, a lot of folks weren't surprised. Mary's family had more money than God, as they say. Wouldn't of been surprised if he'd been having an affair with Mary while engaged to Babs. That's an Ashworth for you. They only think of themselves. They don't know how to love."

Jolene crossed her arms. "That's not true. Robert loves me. I'm sure of it."

"Love isn't twisted like that, Jolene. I loved your mother more than life itself. She led me to the Lord. We only had five years together, and it seemed like she was sick through most of that time. Lost two babies before you came along. She got pneumonia right after. But before she went to the arms of Jesus, she asked me to make peace with Sean Ashworth."

"I take it you didn't have any luck in that regard."

Louise snorted. "Ain't nobody can find a way to make peace with an Ashworth, if you ask me. I might not be from Brookside, but I've lived here long enough to know they're all a bunch of heathens dressed in Armani suits."

Fiddlers Fling

Daddy stroked his beard. "I did try. Visited him after Babs's funeral, like she asked. I think his exact words were, 'I'm going to crush you, Mike Murdock.' Seems like he's spent the last couple of decades trying to make good on that threat."

Jolene met her father's gaze. "Is that why you didn't want me to work for the Ashworths? Why didn't you tell me all this before?"

He turned and stared out the window. "'Cause it wouldn't have made one iota of difference. You'd have bucked no matter what I said. You always had to learn the hard way. Like when I told you not to get too close to the woodstove. You did anyway. Caught you just before you put your hands right on it. Could have scarred you for life."

Her father's words hit home. There'd been enough warnings from the first time she dated Robert in high school. He made fun of everything she loved. What made her believe he'd be any different after they married? If only she could break away before the earth swallowed her whole.

But this was her penance, the cross she'd have to bear, atonement she craved, needed above all else. What did happiness matter?

Chapter Twenty-two

Dwight closed the cover on the portable keyboard while Mahoney put away his guitar. Big Mike and Jolene had just stored their fiddles in their cases when Louise called from the kitchen, "That was so good, I think we oughta celebrate with cake."

Big Mike was the first into the kitchen. Mahoney checked his phone. "Have to pass on the cake, Dwight. Nissie needs a hand with Teddy. She's nursing but pumps out extra so I take a couple of turns with a bottle. Neither one of us is getting much sleep."

Dwight patted Mahoney on the arm. "This too will pass."

"How would you know? Single man like you."

"Don't envy me, Mahoney. I'm the one jealous of you."

"Yeah?"

Dwight glanced toward Jolene. Would he ever be able to move on, find someone else if she married Robert? "I'd like to have a family someday. God's timing, I guess."

Jolene shot him a look like hurtling knives. She looked away, as if unable to meet his gaze.

Mahoney picked up his case and yelled into the kitchen. "Hope you save me a piece for next time, Louise."

She ambled in with two slices on a wrapped plate. "I know the wife's nursing, but a little chocolate cake ain't gonna give your little one a caffeine addiction."

Fiddlers Fling

Mahoney whistled. "You keep feeding us like this and we're going to have to get bigger chairs for the contest."

"And that'd be a crime?" She waddled back into the kitchen.

Jolene picked up her case and moved it by the stairs, with Dwight following close behind. "Found this case in the attic this morning," she said as she turned to look at him, "along with a few photo albums and yearbooks. It was fun going through them. Amazing how the years can change a person."

"Are you so changed you'd refuse a ride on my Raptor? Thought having a little wind on your face might clear your head a little."

"Clear my head of what?"

"This afternoon's conversation with Robert. Sounded pretty heated from my end."

"Not heated at all. Pretty normal, I'd say. Robert always backs down when I stand my ground. He expects it—I deliver. It's a rough ride sometimes, but we always work things out."

"Sounds like a roller-coaster existence if you ask me."

"I'm not asking. As for the Raptor? I'm all in. I hoped I'd get a chance to ride before I return to Albany."

Big Mike poked his head into the living room. "You can take yours, Jolene. Last I knew, it was still running." He turned and walked back out.

"I thought you sold my Raptor." Jolene's eyes bugged as she hurried behind Big Mike, Dwight following once again.

"I kept it. Kept my Summit too, though I haven't ridden it in a few years. Yours is in the far corner, covered with a tarp." Big Mike opened a drawer. "Keys are in here if that Alicia woman hasn't moved them." He rummaged through an assortment of paperwork. "Ah, here they are." He tossed the keys to Jolene. "Be sure to put those back when you're done."

Jolene grinned. "You kept it all. I was worried you sold everything of mine."

"Nearly did when Doc told me the bad news. But something told me not to, even though I'd given up hope you'd ever come back."

Jolene kissed Big Mike on the cheek. "Oh, Daddy, I'm so sorry I didn't come home sooner."

"Blame goes both ways, little girl."

"I know it pains you that I'm still marrying Robert. I promise I'll visit as often as I can. You have to accept him, Daddy. He's not to blame for something his father did."

"I don't blame the boy for the sins of the father. It's that I don't see Robert is much different. He's not right for you." He winked at Dwight.

I can't agree with you more, Big Mike.

Jolene's eyes dulled. "I'll be the judge of who's right for me and who's not. But I don't want it to come between us anymore."

Big Mike put his plate in the sink, usually a sign he was done talking. Instead, he turned to face Jolene. "Guess ain't much I can do on the matter. You're family, Jolene. I won't fight you over the Ashworths ever again."

Dwight put on his cap. "Let's pay your Raptor a visit."

Jolene led the way, hips swaying, her tight-fitting jeans showing off every curve. He reminded himself he shouldn't notice things like that about someone else's fiancée.

She gasped with joy at the Raptor, stored on bricks and covered with care. She pulled back the tarp and ran her slender hands up and down the frame, the dark blue chrome matching her eyes. "Keys are in the ignition," she announced as she mounted.

"Wait! Don't start it yet. Let me check the fuel. "

"I'm not sure I'd remember how to do all that, so go ahead, Sir Galahad."

He checked the fuel line. "There's a little gas left. Big Mike would have known enough to put in an additive. If it's only been a couple of years, the engine should roll over. Let me check the oil."

He puttered a few minutes more, liking the admiration written across Jolene's face, though he knew she eventually would have recalled the whole procedure. The girl knew more about engines than any ten men. "Looks clean. We could take it out for a short spin, if it starts. I'd have Stucky do maintenance on it before you drive it again. Not a better mechanic north of Albany."

"Stucky Bilow?"

"The same."

"I remember him. Is he still as heavy as he was in school?"

"Heavier. Happily married, though. Occasionally plays drums in the worship band. He used to have a major crush on you in high school. Seemed as if most of the boys did. Do you want me to call him?"

Fiddlers Fling

"I know how to use a phone, Dwight. I promise, I'll call." She turned the key, and the Raptor emitted a puff of black smoke.

"Not to worry. That's normal since it's been sitting so long."

After a few minutes of spit and sputter, it stalled.

"Now what?"

"We can ride mine, or try yours after a few minutes."

"I'd like to take mine out if possible."

He leaned against the garage wall. "What do you suppose we do while we wait?"

Jolene dismounted. "I could go for chocolate cake."

"Me too."

Appreciative of Dwight's help, Jolene bit her lower lip, wanting to hug him yet fearful of where it might lead and too vulnerable to resist another kiss. Robert probably sensed Dwight's attraction to her, which is why he had her phone monitored. Next time she went to town, she'd make certain to buy a disposable one. She mentally readied herself for round two of Robert's demands. She'd insist he stop this asinine surveillance, make him see if he continued to treat her this way, there was no hope for a marriage.

She stopped cold when she opened the kitchen door.

Daddy and Louise, standing face-to-face, kissing. He saw her, sat, and held Louise's hand. "Jolene, Dwight, guess you might as well know now. I just proposed to this beautiful woman."

Louise blushed. "I'm as surprised as everyone else. But I said yes."

Chapter Twenty-three

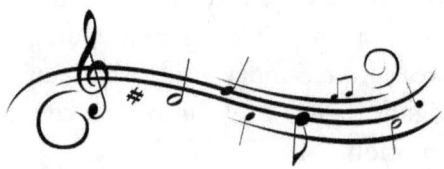

Jolene felt her eyes bug. *Forget the cake.* "Seriously?"

"Absolutely. Louise makes me happy. I like having her around. Why not get married?"

Dwight reddened. "This might be a good time for me to go home. I'll be back with my Raptor." He left, and she realized she'd have to hash this out by herself. Didn't Dwight understand this marriage would affect him too?

An army of questions marched through her mind, but when Jolene opened her mouth, only one word came out: "Louise?"

"I've taken a deep shine to your father. We're not kids, but I think what we have is love. Why not try to bring each other a little happiness in the time your father has left? I plan on taking care of him regardless."

Jolene sat, avoiding the hard questions. What were Louise's expectations about Murdock & Etting? Would Daddy will her the business? Had this been her plan all along when she stepped into his life? Make him dependent on her so she'd get him to marry her? Make her a wealthy widow?

You're just being selfish.

Louise smiled up at Daddy before turning back to Jolene. "I can imagine the worries going through your mind, so I'll put them to rest right off. No, I don't want no part of your father's company. I'll sign a prenup if you want me to. Hard as it may seem, your father and I love each other, but we don't have the luxury of time on our side to go into things slow and easy like."

Fiddlers Fling

Jolene reasoned with them for the next twenty minutes, her efforts to prove the insanity of it all falling on deaf ears. Daddy finally stood and leaned over the table. "My mind is made up, Jolene. Just as yours is. I agreed not to interfere with your marriage to Robert. I expect you to support me in my decision to marry Louise. I don't want to hear any more on the matter."

No sense arguing the matter more. She'd lost. History showed that Murdock against Murdock always ended in a stalemate or one of them leaving. She purposed to stay. "You're right. I'll do what I can to help. Where and when do you plan on having the wedding ceremony?"

"After church, week from Sunday ... if Pastor Tim will do the honors."

The roar of Dwight's Raptor broke into their conversation, and Jolene welcomed the interruption.

Apparently Daddy did too. "Raptor survived storage?"

"Dwight wants me to call Stucky tomorrow and have him give it a tune-up. Otherwise it seems fine."

"Good."

Jolene went to the kitchen door. "We'll talk more when I get back."

"Nothing more to say. You're invited to attend, if you want." He kissed Louise's hand. "This woman will be your stepmother, whether you approve or not."

Dwight waited outside, helmet on, and handed her a second one. He'd already brought her Raptor off the blocks, idling next to his. "Ready?"

"Another reason to make it a short spin. So far I haven't made headway with my father's crazy decision to get married."

"Are you afraid she'll take over Murdock & Etting?"

"She says not. Even willing to sign a prenup."

"If it makes Big Mike happy, why shouldn't they get married?"

"Do I have to have a reason not to be happy about it?"

"No."

She mounted. They rode until Dwight halted at the entrance of the Fish and Game Club, looking toward one trail and then the other. "Where to?"

"Let's take the East. Always was my favorite." Jolene performed a wheelie then sped off in the direction of the forested trail. Dwight raced behind her.

Freedom.

She'd forgotten the thrill of the wind against her face, the purr of the motor underneath—both supports to her soul. At least for the time being, she could ride, and Robert didn't need to know. If he found out, she'd insist on being able to enjoy her Raptor while in Brookside.

She pushed the throttle to full speed. Nature surrounded her, and for a brief time she'd shove aside the abyss of her life and bask in this beautiful moment. She glanced at Dwight, ahead of her by a quarter- mile. Yet against her strong desire otherwise, fear of the future loomed. "Oh, God, how I wish I could find another way to make up for my sin!"

Suddenly, a deer wandered into her path. She spun to the side to avoid a collision, the force of the jar catapulting her out of the vehicle. She rolled until her momentum slowed, then watched helplessly as the Raptor crashed into the row of trees next to the path.

Dwight rushed to her side. "Are you hurt?"

"Mostly my pride." She stood, winced, and fell back down. "Then again, my ankle isn't exactly happy. I don't think it's broken. Maybe sprained."

"Hop on, we'll get you back to the house and put ice on it."

"My Raptor! I want to see how badly it's damaged."

Floodgates opened, and sobs she'd dammed up far too long now broke loose. Crazy she could shed tears for an ATV but not for the life she'd snuffed out. She dismounted, and with Dwight's support, wobbled to the tangled mess of metal and bark.

Dwight lifted her head and met her gaze. "It's a machine, Jolene. I'll help you pick out a new one if you'd like."

"I can buy a new ATV, but I'll never be able to replace this one. It's my childhood, Dwight. It's ... us. I know we can't ever be put back together, but with my hands on the Raptor, the memories, the good times, came alive again. I can't go back, can I? We're forever broken."

Dwight pulled her head to his chest. "Why do you say we can't be fixed? It was a dance. A silly dance. We were kids. We had a fight. Kids do things like that. Why won't you let it go?"

"You don't understand. A ruined prom didn't break us up."

"No? What did?"

Jolene wrenched away from Dwight's hold. "I killed your baby."

Fiddlers Fling

Jolene had been pregnant? When? Why hadn't she told him? Her words ripped through his heart. He'd thought she loved him. You don't abort the seed of someone you love. He must have heard her wrong. There had to be some explanation. Perhaps a miscarriage or something beyond her control. That must be it.

"You were pregnant and never told me?"

"I didn't know until after you left for Fort Jackson. I was scared, so I went to a clinic. I didn't tell anyone. Not even my best friend."

Heat surged through him, anger as he'd never known before. In his heart, he'd forgiven her for running to Robert Ashworth, even blamed himself for driving her to him, his fault she left Brookside. If he hadn't been the fool, he and Jolene would have been married by now. He even fantasized a child or two. Not in his wildest imagination did he believe her capable of aborting his baby.

"Why are you telling me now?"

"I hadn't meant to … ever. This accident … the tangled mess … it's my life … the wreck of what we might have been. And it's my fault."

He wanted to push her to the ground as she struggled to stay upright, to leave her with the smashed Raptor, to forget the benefit tomorrow and the fling in two weeks. How could he keep rehearsing, be close to her knowing she'd betrayed him in the worst possible way?

Jolene searched his eyes, as if wanting him to say she'd been forgiven. He had no words to give her. "Get back on my vehicle. I'll take you home. I'll call Stucky and have him come get your Raptor."

"Then what?"

"Be sure to put ice on that ankle. If the swelling doesn't go down, call Doc Benson in the morning."

Nothing was said as they rode from the Fish and Game Club back to the house. Another moment she couldn't get back, another torrent of guilt. She should never have come home. If she'd listened to Robert and Mother Mary, Dwight would not be in this pain. She'd wounded him in spite of her resolve to keep him ignorant. Better he'd never known than be broken by bitterness. Yet she'd vomited the curt, cruel words.

He pulled his Raptor into the driveway. "Be careful on that ankle."

"Will I see you at church?

"I don't know."

"What about the benefit at the adult center?"

"You and your father can manage without me."

She didn't blame Dwight, but her father would be disappointed. Jolene hobbled into the house, the pain in her ankle mild compared to the ache in her heart. Daddy and Louise sat in the den together, holding hands.

Jolene envied their joy in one another. Was that why she couldn't give her blessing? A resistance birthed from disillusionment? Could love really be simple, complete though destined to be short-lived? Her marriage to Robert would hardly be the stuff of romance novels. Of course she loved Robert; what was there not to admire? A good catch, as the older women would say—rich, successful, and dedicated to the furtherance of mankind. Jolene shuddered with realization. Her commitment to the royal Ashworths had more to do with the queen's determination than the prince's desire. If not influenced by his mother, would he ever have proposed?

Jolene lifted the kitchen curtain and looked out at the darkening sky. Clouds billowed, threatening a severe storm. Much like the mid-July night she'd gone to the pharmacy to pick up a pregnancy test kit. She'd waited until near closing. "For a friend of mine," she told the clerk.

"Is that so?" Mary Ashworth said, stepping up from behind.

Jolene cried and fell into Mary's arms, craving to be cradled, even by the coldest woman in Brookside. She took Jolene by the hand. "Come with me." Mary signaled for Jolene to get into her limo, then rolled up the privacy window. "You may talk freely now."

Jolene cried again, and Mary held her until Jolene's tears were spent. "I'm surprised to see you, Mrs. Ashworth. But thank you for listening, for caring."

"Sean and I are here for a groundbreaking ceremony on a new strip mall. I stopped at the pharmacy for aspirin. I must say, seeing what you bought came as a surprise, you being a good church girl. I assume the father is Dwight?"

Jolene nodded. "I missed my last two periods. I don't know what to do. Dwight and I had a big fight on prom night, and he hasn't talked to me since. I wrote to him, twice, right after he left for Fort Jackson, but he returned my letters unopened. I'm supposed to go to Vassar in the fall."

Funny how desperation can bring two unlikely souls together, to find a dubious friend in the most hated woman in Brookside. They talked for two hours, Mary reassuring, consoling, carefully advising Jolene that abortion was the only reasonable alternative.

Jolene had hesitated. "Dwight would be furious."

"Make sure he never knows."

Mary spelled out the horrors of an unwanted pregnancy and hammered her belief that a woman had a right to decide her own destiny. Jolene relented under the barrage of liberal theology. Mary left the limo for a few minutes. When she returned, she held Jolene's hand. "It's all set, dear. I'll take you to a clinic. You can be home before dawn."

Within the next several hours, Jolene's pregnancy fears were confirmed and terminated. Though filled with remorse, Jolene refused to weep for her loss. She stared out the clinic window as darkness descended. She should have waited, given herself a chance to think the scare through, given Dwight a chance.

Mary held her hand the entire return trip to Brookside. "I understand you think what you did was wrong. That's a normal feeling. It will go away in time." She handed Jolene a book, *The Life and Times of Eleanor Roosevelt*.

"Why are you giving me this?"

"Redemption, if you will. You see, Jolene, you remind me of myself at your age. I too loved a boy who was wrong for me. He was going nowhere, and I wanted to go somewhere. I got pregnant. I took care of the pregnancy but felt empty. When I read this biography of Eleanor Roosevelt, I decided I would spend the rest of my life championing charity. I married Sean Ashworth a few years later."

"You're the source of the Ashworth Foundation?"

"As a wedding present, Sean and I pooled half our trust funds for charity. Perhaps Eleanor will inspire you as she inspired me."

She thanked Mary, then walked into the dark house. Daddy had already gone to bed. She wanted to talk to him, to tell him about the pain bottled up inside. She'd promised Mary to keep the abortion a secret. If Jolene told anyone, she would have implicated Mary too, someone who'd only meant to show Jolene kindness. Unable to sleep, Jolene read the biography from cover to cover. Afterward, she knew beyond any doubt she would become a social worker. She could not undo the sin, but if she worked hard to make the world a better place, perhaps God would forgive her. She would work as hard as she could toward that end.

Jolene turned away from the kitchen window, wearied from the resurrected memory of Mary Ashworth's influence that night. Through a new perspective, she now knew the truth. She had been manipulated at a time when she'd been the most vulnerable. The question that played in her mind now was why … what motive had Mary Ashcroft possessed in her pretentious compassion?

Jolene limped into the den. "Daddy, something's come up and Dwight won't be able to play for either the benefit Sunday or the contest. We might as well drop out. I don't think we'll do as well without the keyboard."

Daddy studied her. "What's wrong with your ankle, little girl? You're limping." He frowned. "You two have a fight?"

"I don't want to talk about it." She choked back the threatening new stream of tears. "I'm going back to Albany tomorrow."

"Will you come home for my wedding?"

"You really intend to get married?"

Daddy and Louise nodded in sync.

"You're both crazy, you know."

Daddy smiled. "Might be, but it's my choice to be crazy, isn't it?"

"I'll be there. I'm going upstairs to pack."

She took the steps, avoiding the tendency to put weight on her injured ankle, then opened the door to her old room. Her future, if she had one, could only be found in Albany. She tucked her jeans and tee into the dresser, along with her picture of Dwight. She picked up her fiddle and played two measures of "Orange Blossom Special" but was unable to finish, disappointment more than she could bear.

She emptied the contents of her temporary handbag to repack in the purse Mother Mary had given her. She couldn't return to Albany with a cheap knockoff.

As she searched the room, panic seized her. She must have left her ring at the Ashworth mansion. Mother Mary would definitely notice if Jolene returned without it. She'd have to go back to the mansion and look there. She grabbed her car keys. In her rush, she'd forgotten to baby her ankle and dashed down the steps, hit with crippling pain at the bottom stair. She forced herself out the door and to the car , hobbling like an amputee without a crutch.

Fiddlers Fling

Could she even drive? In sports, she'd pushed through worse pain than this. She could do it again. She prayed. "I've messed up again, God. Show me what's right ... by Daddy and Robert, as well as Dwight."

She pulled into the circular driveway. Expecting to be only a few minutes, she once again left the car running. She hurried into the house just as a bright burst of lightening skittered across the sky, followed by a deafening thunderclap, announcing an imminent storm.

Climbing the main stairwell brought excruciating pain. When she returned home, she'd take Dwight's advice and wrap a bag of ice around her ankle. She'd finish packing in the morning. At the landing, she heard muffled voices, laughter and then silence. Probably her imagination since, back in the day, this house would have made a perfect setting for a Vincent Price movie.

She found her purse and engagement ring in the drawer where she'd stuffed it a few days ago. Retreating in haste, she collided with Alicia Davenport, dressed only in a sheer negligee, backing out from the room next to where Jolene had slept.

"Alicia?"

"Jolene! I thought you were staying at your father's." She glanced toward the room she'd just exited.

"A little early for sleeping, isn't it?" Disgust mixed with curiosity. Robert had told Jolene that Alicia frequently stayed at the Ashworth mansion. No surprise that she was here tonight. However, who was the man of the hour behind her door? The catty remarks would have to wait. Just then, Robert, hair uncombed and his opened silk robe revealing his manhood, stepped from Alicia's room into the hall.

Alicia tossed her hair back. "Robert, I believe you have company."

Jolene froze in disbelief. Yet there had been more than enough sirens to warrant suspicion. She'd been gullible enough to ignore them, trusting enough to believe Robert loved only her. "How could you?"

His gaze, devoid of remorse, burned. "Alicia, dear, go ask the butler to put out our supper while I talk to Jolene."

She left, making no effort to improve her lack of modesty, apparently comfortable strutting through the mansion like a Victoria Secret model.

"I have nothing to say, Robert." Jolene threw her engagement ring at his feet along with the hated handbag.

"Jolene, don't be brash. This isn't what you think."

"Oh, really?"

"Alicia means nothing to me. I still want to marry you."

"And that makes your betrayal okay? Well ... here's a news flash. The wedding of the year is off. I'll never marry you. Not after this." Her heart raced, but she could manage only a fast limp down the steps and out the door, breaking every speed limit back to her father's house.

Her cell rang as she pulled into the driveway. She parked and checked the caller ID. Mary Ashworth. No more Mother Mary ... no more cowering at the feet of Her Majesty. This time Jolene would tell the Ice Queen exactly what her former future daughter-in-law thought.

"This is Jolene."

"Robert told me what happened and that you broke off your engagement. Don't you think you're being a bit hasty?"

"Are you actually condoning Robert's behavior?"

"Of course not, dear. But you need to understand. Ashworth men are weak when it comes to women. Their infidelity doesn't mean they don't love their wives. Goodness knows, Sean has had his share of affairs. Most successful men do. FDR was included in the fraternity of men who seek out a harem of admiring lovers, but his wife forgave him. Do you consider yourself more righteous than Eleanor?"

Reality left Jolene breathless. "As I've recently been told, I'm *not* Eleanor Roosevelt. I refuse to allow Robert, or any man for that matter, to humiliate me ever again. Call me old-fashioned, but I expect a husband to be faithful, a trait, by your own admission, Robert lacks."

"Let's be reasonable, dear. Breaking your engagement with my son will not go well for you."

A threat?

"So be it." Jolene disconnected.

Why hadn't she seen Mary's agenda until now? Like jagged puzzle pieces, Jolene put together the decade-long manipulations. Her first date with Robert had been his prom, the details of the event arranged by his mother, right down to Jolene's gown. At the time, she'd imagined herself a Cinderella, with a prince on her arm. He'd been attentive, polite, took her home when the dance ended, walked her to the door, and kissed her ... a kiss with no hint of desire. Yet she swelled with pride to have been the interest of the most popular boy in Brookside.

Fiddlers Fling

After a few dates, lunch together in the school cafeteria, and holding hands in the hall, she and Robert became a Brookside High item. But he left for Harvard, and she fell in love with Dwight Etting, her thoughts rarely floating toward Robert except when she'd run into Mary. Though they owned several estates, Mary managed to spend a great deal of time in Brookside for this event or the other. Jolene hadn't realized until now the odd places she'd run into Robert's mother: the library, the music store, and Barkman's Hardware. Mary never failed to strike up a conversation with Jolene, particularly to ask what her post-school plans might be. In retrospect, Jolene pondered the improbable. Had she been groomed by Robert's mother as her son's future wife ... even then?

For what purpose?

There were far richer fields to farm than the heir of Murdock and Etting. Or could Mother Mary have snared the daughter of Brookside's most prominent political influence?

"Hell hath no fury like a woman scorned," the bard said. Jolene straightened her shoulders with energized determination. She was Big Mike Murdock's daughter. Someone who could not be bought or intimidated. Not any longer. Not even by Mary Ashworth.

Chapter Twenty-four

Most Sundays, Dwight looked forward to church servicew, considering his part in the worship band a privilege. Congregants filed in, perhaps some anticipating a special encounter with the Lord. Would his hypocrisy interfere with their expectation? Maybe he should have called Pastor Tim and bailed.

After praise-team warmup, Dwight flexed his fingers. Pastor Tim had selected several rousing numbers, including "Let the Veil Down," one of Dwight's favorites, the words suggesting nothing should interfere with worship … not anger, nor its shadowy cousin, resentment.

Yet bile from Jolene's confession still burned his insides.

He stood as Mahoney came up behind him, his guitar strapped around his shoulder. Jack, Dwight's ever-true friend, the man who'd put a tourniquet on his leg, carried him through battle and out of harm's way to hand him over to a medic. Though a higher rank, Mahoney had saluted Dwight. "Get that taken care of, buddy. We have lots of fighting ahead of us."

Prophetic words, never more true than the last week.

"What time is the benefit today?" Mahoney asked.

"Four o'clock, but I don't think I'll make it."

"That so?" Mahoney rested his guitar on a stand and glanced at his watch. "We've got fifteen minutes before service starts. I could use a stretch. Might wake me up. Had an all-nighter with Teddy."

Fiddlers Fling

They left the sanctuary by way of the side entrance on to Main Street. Mahoney's clip matched Dwight's, but neither offered conversation until they reached the intersection. Mahoney arched a brow. "So, care to share what's wrong?"

"Why do think something's wrong?"

"You were looking forward to the benefit. I suspect a pretty blonde is behind your change in tune."

Dwight stopped, picked up a twig, tossed it toward a nearby lawn, and continued walking. "Sometimes I think you know me better than I know myself. The day I got shot, you sensed I'd sooner die."

"Faith gave you a will to live. What about now?"

"Life's gotten a little complicated."

"Faith can fix that too."

"Maybe."

"No maybe about it. What happened?"

Could he tell Mahoney without owning guilt? "We should be getting back."

Mahoney saluted. "I outrank you. Out with it, soldier."

Dwight sighed. Might as well plunge into the deep part of the pool. "Seems Jolene kept a humdinger of a secret from me."

"Don't most women?"

"Not like this one. She had no right."

"Enough mystery. The door's cracked. Now open it so we won't be late for worship."

"She had an abortion."

"Ouch. Yours?"

Dwight nodded.

"When?

"Summer of our senior year, but she never told me until last night. If she loved me, how could she have done a thing like that?"

"She was a pregnant kid and scared."

"Not a good enough excuse. If she'd told me, I'd have come home. We could have gotten married. We were young, but we would have managed."

"Dwight, are you sure she didn't try to tell you?"

"Yeah."

Dwight raked his hair with sudden remembrance. "She wrote me a couple of letters soon after I arrived at Fort Jackson. I sent them both back ... unopened. You don't think ..."

"Only God knows. But if she tried to tell you, and you sent the letters back, she was probably frightened out of her wits. I'm not justifying what she did, but her actions weren't much different than any kid in those circumstances."

"You know, we were both brought up in church. We shouldn't have found ourselves in that situation."

"Life happens, even to church kids. We don't inherit a relationship with the Lord. That has to happen personally. You didn't get your act together until a Taliban soldier put a bullet in your thigh. Maybe Jolene has yet to find a real relationship with the Lord."

"I hate that you're always right." Dwight opened the side door and stepped into the sanctuary and made his way to the platform. *Am I supposed to forgive her, Lord? How can I?*

Jolene took her place in the pew next to her father. Funny to see Daddy and Louise holding hands like a couple of teenagers. He used to tap Dwight on the shoulder when he sat too close to Jolene during services and motioned for the two of them to slide apart.

The curious heads that turned when the Murdocks walked into the sanctuary now faced forward. The song leader signaled the congregation to rise while the words flashed on the viewer. "Let the Veil Down."

Jolene knew her veils were numerous, most of her own doing. She listened as the congregation sang, hands waving, hearts rejoicing. Like the father she remembered, a man who loved God and worshiped without reservation, Daddy raised his hands toward heaven.

She'd grown up with the old hymns and praise songs the youth team sang. She'd stood on the platform, but the hands she raised had been unholy, meant to impress others, not from a true relationship with God. She'd heard the sinner's prayer, could recite the words, remembering how congregates knelt in sorrow while the praise team sang, "Just as I Am." They'd come broken to be mended, and the Lord met them there at an altar of contrition. Though her music led others, she herself had never followed—easier to pretend, to recite the familiar words she'd heard from infancy. Her father, on the other hand, lived what he believed—until their argument. He'd lost his way, but God brought him back—more like he'd been detoured. In her case, she never had a way to lose. No wonder she'd fallen into Mary Ashworth's trap.

Her sin was great, her abortion, not a mistake but rather a deliberate choice. Yet the greater sin was that she had turned to Mary Ashworth as her savior, instead of to the Lord.

A presence surrounded her as the song implied. As the congregation lifted their praise, she cracked the veil that had separated her from the hope she'd ignored. *You brought me back to my earthly father. Now I ask that you bring me home to you.*

Peace reigned—heartache fled.

Forgiven by her father, forgiven by her Lord.

As for Dwight, she had no control over his decision to forgive her or not. Rough waters stretched ahead. Whatever her future brought, the journey began here, submitted to God's sovereignty.

A new set of words flashed on the screen, words from an old hymn she used to sing with Daddy … "I Need Thee Every Hour."

She sang from her forgiven heart.

When the worship set finished, Jolene glanced toward Dwight as he walked down the opposite aisle and out of the building.

Chapter Twenty-five

Dwight strode from the church with long, purposeful strides, wanting to run to the parking lot and slouch inside his truck to think. He couldn't stay for the sermon, his rebellious spirit too restless.

He was pleased to see Big Mike and Louise, glad Mike had this good woman in his life to provide comfort when Jolene returned to Albany. Dwight tried to pray, but thoughts weren't lofty enough.

Forgive Jolene.

I know I should. I can't, Lord

Can't ... or won't?

If he forgave her or not, company business demanded he keep the relationship afloat. Though she'd made Dwight CEO, she'd never be satisfied as a silent partner. He could only avoid her by leaving Brookside.

What was he thinking? He could no more turn his back on Murdock & Etting than he could his faith. As a foreman, Mahoney was the best, but only Dwight would be able to see the new contracts through to completion. Brookside needed the economic boost. If he left, Ashworth won again.

A loud rap against the window startled him. What was *she* doing in the church parking lot? Was she still following him? Alicia Davenport was many things he disliked, but he never pegged her as a stalker.

He rolled down his window, and she stuck her head through the opening, her black hair falling over her right shoulder, her perfume strong but strangely intoxicating, alluring. How could someone so vile smell so good?

Fiddlers Fling

"If you're here for services, you're a half-hour late."

"And you're leaving a half-hour early."

Before he could object, she opened the passenger door and climbed in.

"What do you want, Alicia? If it's about Ashworth's campaign, I've told you more times than I can count, I will not support his candidacy."

"I'm here on Robert's behalf, true, but this is not about his campaign."

"Since when do you use the words Robert and campaign and not equate the two?"

She laughed, her cackle like a hyena with a sore throat, the second reason he stopped dating her. "You haven't heard, I take it."

Alicia loved to torque suspense. She should be a novelist.

"Heard what?"

"Jolene broke off her engagement to Robert. Mary Ashworth blames you. She's livid."

Alicia pulled out an envelope and tossed it toward Dwight. "You're being sued. Consider yourself served."

"On what grounds?"

"Defamation of character." She opened the door and slid out.

"That's a load of crap."

"Is it?" She slammed the passenger door and sashayed out of sight.

Dwight positioned his keyboard next to Mahoney's guitar. He gazed at the building, but no sign of Jolene or Big Mike. Mahoney talked with the center's manager, Tammy Winston, and both waved in acknowledgment of Dwight's arrival.

He'd convinced himself to come today, partly because a dying child didn't deserve his benefit to fizzle and partly to let the Ashworths know Dwight Etting wouldn't be scared away by another lawsuit.

A former boarding school built at the turn of the century, Brookside Senior Center buzzed with visitors, an appearance by Jolene and Big Mike Murdock garnering front-page publicity.

Big Mike and Louise entered from the rear door with Jolene who limped slightly behind them. He met Jolene's gaze, her eyes swollen, her cheeks sallow. "Thank you for showing up, Dwight. Took a lot of courage. I don't blame you if you're still angry with me."

"I'm here for Big Mike and the kid."

She turned away before he could ask the question ... what had happened between her and Robert?

Mahoney placed a list of songs on Dwight's keyboard. "Since we weren't sure you were coming, Big Mike asked me to finalize today's repertoire. Take note of some last-minute changes Jolene requested."

Dwight glanced at the arrows and cross-outs. "We're opening and closing with Jolene's solos?"

Mahoney nodded. "If you're not sure of the lineup, glance my way, and I'll mouth the next one. Jolene asked for the first number to be done *a cappella* after Jolene's solos on the first two verses. If you take bass, I'll do the tenor. Big Mike will pluck the fiddle toward the end."

"Got it."

"Watch me for key changes. BTW, glad you swallowed your pride enough to make it. The Callahan family thanks you too."

"Like I told Jolene, I'm here for Big Mike as well as the kid."

"Tammy will make the announcement later, but word is Joshua's next in line for his heart transplant. Crazy, isn't it? A heart will only become available if someone dies. How do you pray for something like that?"

"Pray knowing God's in control."

"Speaking for yourself or Josh Callahan?"

Dwight signaled Tammy that the group was ready to begin. She introduced each band member, congratulating Mahoney on the new baby, to which he received a well-deserved standing ovation. "And we're blessed to have Jolene Murdock, fiancée of senatorial hopeful Robert Ashworth."

Apparently the breakup hadn't made headlines yet.

"And of course, we're doubly blessed with the duet magic of Jolene and Big Mike Murdock."

As the applause thundered, Jolene took the microphone. "Thank you for your resounding welcome. I'm sure you'll recognize this song from the soundtrack of *O Brother, Where Art Thou?*

Tears welled as she began to sing, "Down to the River to Pray," power and conviction in her vocals. Something had happened to her, something only God could orchestrate.

Except for Big Mike, each band member sang either a hymn or a favorite country song. To audience cheers, Big Mike finished off the group efforts by taking the lead with "Orange Blossom Special." To the audience's wild approval, Mahoney played "It is Well with My Soul" on his steel guitar.

Fiddlers Fling

Jolene introduced her last vocal, dedicated to the Callahan family. "We don't know why suffering and uncertainty come into our lives," she said. "But we can trust the one who understands each tear that falls." She sang "Amazing Grace" to a hushed audience.

Dwight thought of the whirlwind of the last week, how he imagined himself still in love with Jolene. She'd been right. He'd loved the memory of her. The woman she'd become was a stranger. She was still Big Mike's daughter and would be chief partner when Big Mike was gone. Avoidance was not an option. At the least, he could rejoice in her decision not to marry Ashworth.

Jolene breathed a heavy sigh when the last of the benefit crowd left. Louise and Daddy hugged her goodbye. "We're on our way now, dear. Hurry home," Louise said, already assuming her upcoming role of stepmother. "I got beef stew in the crockpot."

She hadn't spoken to anyone about ending her engagement. Since Tammy didn't know, Jolene assumed the tabloids hadn't published the news that Robert Ashworth was once again the most eligible bachelor in New York.

Dwight's attention seemed focused on Tammy as they huddled in conversation at the other end of the building. Dwight leaned against the wall, exuding his boyish charm. Heat surged. Jealousy or protectiveness? Why shouldn't he be interested in Tammy? Pretty, single, and not a bad singer ... someone who hadn't betrayed him.

She felt a rush of uncertainty, her immediate future a huge question mark. Where would she live when her father and Louise married? They'd want their privacy. Though grateful for a small savings, money would quickly become a problem. She'd have to find a job soon or go to work for Murdock & Etting. Not a good option if she had to face Dwight every day. And with most of the local human services organizations financially indebted to the Ashworth Foundation, Brookside held few employment prospects for someone in disfavor with the Ashworths.

She sighed. Answers would come in God's time.

She picked up her fiddle case and headed for the south exit just as Alicia Davenport entered the building and approached with unparalleled audacity. "If you'd answer your texts, I wouldn't have to hunt you down like this."

You sleep with my fiancé, then act as if I'm the one who inconvenienced you? Remembering she was in a public place, Jolene mustered restraint. "I suggest you leave immediately, or I'll file a harassment complaint against you."

Alicia laughed, a controlled cackle, but to Jolene's ear, as irritating as a she-devil on steroids. "I have a message from Mary."

"Not interested." Jolene tried to leave, but Alicia blocked the exit.

"Oh, but you should be." She tilted her head to the side and crossed her arms, a human *tsk*. "Dwight didn't tell you?"

"Tell me what?"

"Robert's suing him for defamation of character."

"That's insane."

"Not so. You really didn't think your phone was private, did you? All those conversations with Dwight?"

Mary would continue to badger and manipulate until the Ashworth's had destroyed everything her father had accomplished, including his child. Daddy still wielded a lot of political influence in Brookside. Did she think by attacking the heiress, their nemesis would go silently into that dark night?

Robert needed to carry Brookside to win the state senatorial district. As a junior partner, Dwight rose to become as much a Brookside political force as Big Mike Murdock.

Alicia clicked her tongue. "Mary's very worried about Robert. He's distressed that you ended your engagement. Believe it or not, he does truly love you."

"Fine way of showing it."

"You're so naïve, Jolene. True, Robert beds other women, but you're the one he wants to marry."

"Not the kind of marriage I want."

"Eleanor Roosevelt accepted FDR's infidelity, understood his weakness. Look at what great things they accomplished ... separately and together. Think of all the opportunities for good you're throwing away simply because of some puritanical nonsense that a husband must be faithful in order to have a successful marriage."

Fiddlers Fling

"That puritanical nonsense you flippantly refer to is my spiritual rock. I can't live by any other code."

"Where was that code when you had your abortion?"

Alicia knew too? An inner restraint, perhaps a Holy Ghost straightjacket, prevented Jolene from planting a right hook on Alicia's chin. Jolene wasn't the same desperate girl she'd been seven years ago, without Light to guide her. "At that time, I wasn't a true believer. I am now. My mind is set. The engagement is over."

Alicia straightened from her unnatural bend. "Well, Jolene, digest this. Mary is prepared to make your abortion public record. The good people of Brookside will resent you. We can drag the lawsuit against Dwight out for a long time. When word gets out that Brookside's beloved son fathered a child that was ultimately aborted, he'll lose all credibility. Robert will appear the victim. And what do you think the publicity will do to your father? He'll die of heartbreak before the cancer takes him."

Jolene shivered as fear gripped her. What had she done? She'd broken her engagement in a spirit of rebellion, a selfish burst of anger. What if her haste harmed those she loved?

She must get home. She'd tell Daddy before Mary Ashworth could make good her threat. Jolene hurried to the parking lot, turning in circles, her eyes scanning the nearly empty lot, not quite believing her car was missing.

Dwight excused himself from his conversation with Tammy, who asked if the group could perform again next month. Too far in advance to make the commitment for Big Mike. Who was to say? Since he stopped drinking, found love and purpose again, he might outlive Doc Benson's predictions.

As Dwight readied his keyboard, female voices near the south exit caught his attention. Jolene and Alicia seemed in some sort of heated debate. Alicia had no business being here. Bad enough she'd threatened Dwight. What did she think she could do to Jolene?

Alicia left and Jolene exited soon after. Whatever the argument, it must be over. He loaded the keyboard onto the truck and returned for the rest of his equipment. Jolene stood in the back of the building pounding the daylights out of her cell.

Did she have any idea the sensuality she oozed when befuddled?

He made his way toward her. "If you hit that phone any harder, it'll fly out of your hands. Something wrong?"

"For one thing, my car is missing."

"Missing? As in stolen?"

"More like the Ashworths probably towed it away. It was a rental, under Sean's name."

"Why would they do that?"

"No need for the dumb act. Alicia told me you know I broke my engagement to Robert."

"Looks like they aren't wasting any time to retaliate."

Her lips parted in a thin smile. "Be careful what you say about the Ashworths from now on. Alicia just told me your head's on the chopping block too."

"Like, I'm really scared. Come on, I'll take you home. Wouldn't leave you stranded."

"Will you stay for dinner? Louise said she has beef stew in the crockpot. I'm sure there's plenty."

"Sure." If Ashworth had some agenda toward him, it also involved Jolene. They'd have to work together to save the company.

As they made their way toward the truck, Jolene tossed her cell into the outside trash bin.

"You're throwing away your iPhone?"

"My service was through the Ashworths. I see they wasted no time in stopping that too. Looks like the fun is just getting started."

Chapter Twenty-six

Jolene leaned back against the dining room chair and pushed her bowl into the center of the table. Louise's beef stew proved beyond any doubt which woman was the better cook. "I surrender, Louise."

She laughed. "Didn't know we were in a contest."

"I'll confess. I like to cook and used to be pretty good at it, even as a teenager. But I can't come close to your expertise. Where did you learn culinary art like this?"

Louise cackled. "Not really a secret, so I don't mind telling you. I used to be a chef. I quit when I got married."

Jolene smiled. "Too bad you quit. You could have been a wife *and* a chef."

"Not according to my husband. Besides, I liked looking after our home and cooking only for him."

"That explains why everything you make tastes so good."

"God gives each of us gifts and talents, Jolene. I can carry a tune, but I'd never be able to sing or play the fiddle like you. Whatever talents we're blessed with, he expects us to use for his glory. I like to serve the Lord with my cooking."

Daddy chuckled. "You two gals act like a man has to choose whose cooking he prefers over the other. You're both good."

Subdued until now, Dwight joined the group in laughter.

Fiddlers Fling

Daddy pushed his bowl aside, his smile vanished, his face taut. "Before we settle in for Louise's Red Velvet Cake, we need to have a conversation about a couple of things."

Growing up, her father's "conversation" usually amounted to a lecture or an edict, most often both, and always one-sided with no room for rebuttal. "A conversation? Like the kind I had as a little girl?"

"Somewhat. Got a call from Mary Ashworth today."

Jolene stared at Dwight. "About what?"

"Don't know when you were going to tell me about young Ashworth. Not that I'm unhappy."

The retelling of Robert's betrayal brought fresh tears. "I've done a lot of things in my life I wish I hadn't. I've asked forgiveness for them all. I can learn to forgive Robert in time, but that doesn't mean I have to marry him."

Daddy smirked. "Kind of thought it might be something like that. Glad you figured out the real him before you tied the knot. Listen, little girl, not all men need fulfillment outside the marriage bed. You deserve better. All I ever wanted for you was to be the person God intended you to be. The special you he created ... not some hoity-toity Ashworth makeover."

Jolene hesitated. How much about Dwight's predicament should she reveal? "I see that now, but I'm still worried. Mary Ashworth is determined to be spiteful. I don't see what she would gain by hurting us."

Dwight shrugged his shoulders. "For some reason, Big Mike, she's after me too. Robert has served me with a lawsuit, blaming me for defaming his good name. Doesn't need me for that—he does a pretty good job looking like an idiot without my help."

"There's something else." Daddy trembled, and Louise patted his hand. "Something Jolene went through the summer after graduation. I thought I should keep this private, just me and Jolene. Louise knows, but this concerns Dwight too."

Dwight nodded. "Jolene told me yesterday."

Jolene gasped. "You know, Daddy?"

"I knew a long time ago."

"How?"

"Dwight, remember the letters from Jolene you returned unopened? A father does things he shouldn't when he worries about a daughter. Jolene had been so melancholy, I thought maybe the letter might shed light. I opened it and found out my little girl was worried she might be pregnant with your baby."

"You must have been mad enough to kill me."

"Thought did cross my mind. Good thing for you I was a Christian man, and you were away at training camp, serving your country. I resealed everything and put it on Jolene's dresser. I thought I'd wait and talk to her when she was sure." Tears wet his cheeks as he turned toward Jolene. "I should have talked to you right then and there. I waited, thinking you'd tell me eventually."

Dwight's eyes widened. "How did you find out about the abortion?"

"Bert called me after his daughter waited on Jolene at the drugstore. Said she bought a pregnancy test. Said he thought he should let me know, one father to another. He saw Jolene leave with Mary Ashworth. Later she called, offering a bribe for him to keep quiet. He refused. By the time I tracked Jolene down, the clinic told me it was too late."

"I can't believe you never said anything to me."

"No point, Jolene. I couldn't change what happened."

Quiet until now, Dwight stood and walked to the window. "Jolene, what was the name of the clinic you went to?"

"I don't remember. Everything happened so fast. I was upset, and I didn't pay much attention. I don't think the place was very far from Brookside. Took about half an hour to get there."

"Bakersfield?"

"Might have been."

"Name Fremont Clinic ring any bells?"

Jolene caught her breath. "Yes, I think that was the name of the place. Why?"

"Got a hunch." He pulled out his cell and punched in a number. A pause, then, "Hi, Nissie ... Dwight Etting ... No, I'm not calling for Jack. I want to talk to you. Got a minute?"

After another pause, Dwight said, "I know what I'm asking you might be confidential information, but I need to confirm a suspicion about the Fremont Clinic. Do you mind if I put you on speaker? I'm with some people who need to hear this."

Dwight clicked on the speaker just as Nissie said, "Don't let any girls you know go there."

"Why's that?"

"I'll deny I told you this, but Fremont Clinic is under investigation for fraudulent medical procedures."

"You mean abortions?"

"Allegedly, mind you, they scammed a lot of young, frightened girls who came in thinking they were pregnant. They performed unwarranted D & Cs and passed them off as abortions, charging the girls sky-high fees. Poor dears were so heavily drugged they didn't know what was or wasn't done to them. Makes me so mad."

"No court action pending?"

"District Attorney Landreau is having a hard time building a case."

"Why's that?"

"Besides the fact no one will come forward to testify, Mary Ashworth has chaired Fremont Clinic's Board for the last ten years."

"That explains a great deal."

"Why are you asking, Dwight?"

"I can't tell you right now. Please know the information is very important to us, and of course, we'll keep everything you told us under our hats."

"I'm not too worried about that. Most of what I told you has been Bakersfield gossip for years. If you find out anything that can help Cedric's case, let him know."

"I'll do that. Thanks again, Nissie."

"Glad I can help."

Dwight disconnected and turned to Jolene. "Did you hear her okay?"

Jolene nodded. "If what Nissie says is true, is there a possibility I was never pregnant?"

Dwight met her gaze, his face red as if anger consumed him. "Jolene, I think you and I should pay Doc Benson a visit tomorrow."

"Good idea, Dwight." Daddy, who never quoted a book except his own version of scripture, leaned back in his chair. "The Bard said it best: 'Something ain't right in Denmark.'"

Chapter Twenty-seven

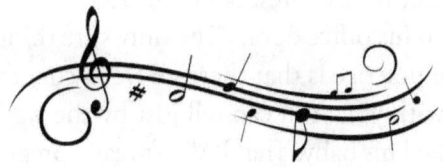

Doc Benson closed the door to his private office while Dwight waited in the lobby. "I'd like to do more extensive blood work at the hospital. Looks as though you're Rh negative, something you should know if you ever do become pregnant."

"Are you implying I never was?"

"If you had been, even with early termination, there'd be a bubble in the cervix. There's no evidence of any pregnancy. I do see there's some vaginal scarring as if you had a D & C performed. I suspect, if you went to that clinic in Bakersfield, it's possible they falsified the pregnancy test and performed the procedure to make you think you had an abortion. Whether Mary Ashworth was aware they performed an unwarranted procedure on you, I don't know. But I can assure you, you were never pregnant."

Joy mingled with new guilt. She was glad she hadn't actually terminated a pregnancy, yet she had undergone a procedure with that intent. Her condemnation remained the same—perhaps a little easier to forgive herself, but still undeserving of God's forgiveness, though freely given. Surprisingly, peace settled over her.

"Thank you, Doctor Benson."

"For what it's worth, Jolene, I'm glad you broke off your engagement with young Ashworth. That life would have swallowed you like Jonah in the whale's belly."

"No one's sure the fish that swallowed Jonah was actually a whale."

"Doesn't matter. He was still swallowed and was probably scarred for life when the fish threw him up."

Doc Benson, a childhood fixture, towered with majesty in Jolene's eyes. She remembered his explanations and lectures, especially when she contracted mononucleosis. He had made her promise that she and Dwight give up kissing for a while.

Jolene shifted in her chair, the whole exam and results disquieting. "I'll follow up on those blood tests, Doctor Benson, although a wedding and baby are definitely not in my foreseeable future."

He walked her to his office door. "The only sure thing I've learned in all my years of medical practice is that there's never a sure thing. Dwight's still very much in love with you. You can tell just by the way he looks at you."

"He thinks I killed his baby. That I wasn't really pregnant doesn't change the fact I was willing to do just that."

"He might come around yet. You were a kid, impressionable and influenced by an adult who pretended to care. In my book, Mary Ashworth deserves more blame than you."

"Maybe. The way I see it, we're each responsible for the choices we make. Excusing them or putting the blame elsewhere doesn't change that truth. All that matters is, God has forgiven me."

Doc Benson clicked his tongue, a usual preface to instruction. "I hope you'll report this, Jolene. I'll sign whatever Cedric needs. There's a long line of doctors who would like to see Fremont Women's Clinic shut down for good."

Jolene came into the lobby, her expression unreadable. Dwight put the magazine he'd been reading on the side table. Should he push for information? Maybe the news was bad—bad enough she didn't want to share."

"Ready?"

She nodded and he led the way to his truck. Once on the road, she glanced his way. "Thank you for coming with me."

"I have a stake in all this too."

"I was never pregnant."

Did that change anything between them? "I thought so."

"Doc Benson wants me to file a complaint with Cedric Landreau."

"You should."

Jolene stared out the passenger window. Pregnant or not, she'd gone to the clinic willingly, intent on taking the life of his baby. She still betrayed him. This much he did understand—kids make stupid decisions, and he had a long list of regrets too. God didn't place sins on a bell curve. Weren't his as great as Jolene's in God's eyes? The Lord had wiped both slates clean, and in some ways Dwight had been in need of a greater dose of grace.

"You're pretty deep in thought, Jolene."

"There's nothing more to say. I have to move forward, Dwight. Lots of decisions to make, and I don't have the luxury of time."

"Do you know where you'll live?"

"Daddy and Louise want me to stay at the house. Makes sense. He's already becoming weaker. It won't be long before Louise will need help with his care. I want to be there for them."

"Anything I can do?"

"I need to rent a vehicle. The Raptor's still in the shop. Besides, I don't think I should go job hunting on an ATV, and I can't expect Louise and you to cart me everywhere I need to go."

"Stucky has a few cars in his lot he keeps for loaners. He might rent one to you. Otherwise, the nearest rental places are in Bakersfield. I could take you there tomorrow."

"You've got a business to manage. I'm counting on you to get those new contracts started."

Dwight sat up straighter, one good thing amidst all the recent upheaval. "We're making progress. Mayor Billings called this morning and scheduled a groundbreaking ceremony next week for the nursing home project."

"Of all the craziness since I came back to Brookside, at least I did one thing right when I made you CEO."

"You've done a lot of things right. Somehow God will bring good out of all this mess."

"What did the man with the sick daughter say about believing?"

"I believe ... help my unbelief."

"Not even Alicia could spin this for good."

"You gotta have faith."

Jolene snickered. "I've been a church girl my whole life. I've been a Christian only one day. I don't know if I have that kind of faith just yet."

"I'll have to have enough for the both of us."

Fiddlers Fling

Her beautiful smile, like sun after a week of rain, warmed his heart, but forgiving her still seemed beyond his grasp.

"Drop me off at Stucky's. I'll get back ... home ... from there."

"There's no rush, is there?"

Her eyes widened with wild determination as the truth hit Dwight, nearly sucking the air from his lungs.

"Why? You're not planning on confronting Mary Ashworth on your own, are you?"

"Whatever I plan on doing, I can handle myself, thank you very much." Jolene sighed. For what she intended, best Dwight was kept in the dark.

He parked in front of Stucky's and leaned back against the seat. "I'll wait until I'm sure Stucky has a vehicle for you. I'd feel better if I weren't worried you're going to Bakersfield tomorrow."

"Don't worry about me so much. Besides, I have errands to run. I promised Louise I'd arrange a reception at the house after their wedding Sunday. You've done more than enough."

Stucky's Garage was as much in disarray as its owner, tools spread from one end of the shop to the other, rags heaped in a corner, kerosene stench so strong Jolene's stomach flip-flopped.

"Jolene?" She jumped at Stucky's voice behind her.

"I stopped by to check on the Raptor."

"I already told you it'd be another couple of days."

"I'm amazed you could salvage it."

"You didn't come here about the ATV. I see Dwight's waiting for you in the truck. What's going on?"

"I need to rent a car. Dwight thought you might have one I could use."

"I have a Subaru might work for you. In good shape." He winked. "No charge. I heard about your breakup. Least I can do."

"I insist on paying." She whipped out a debit card, the one from her private account. "This should be good."

He ran it through his computer as he stretched his jaw. "Um ... do you have a different one?"

"Rejected?"

He nodded.

"You're kidding."

"Wish I were."

Jolene slapped the counter. "Why, those ... " She couldn't finish without using language that would make even Stucky blush. Mary or Robert must have gone through her apartment, found bank statements, and compromised her private account.

Stucky wiped his hands with a greasy rag. "I'm sure it's all a misunderstanding. Take the car and pay me when you get things straightened out."

Two days ago, she casually worried about an expensive purse. Now her survival depended upon the mercy of others.

Stucky grabbed a set of keys. "I'll gas it up for you. Only be a minute."

Jolene waved Dwight on and sat in the waiting area, surprised to see clean chairs and a coffee table loaded with *Popular Mechanic* magazines. Stucky had always had a capacity for kindness. She warmed with embarrassment to remember how badly she teased him for bringing his Bible to school every day.

Within thirty minutes, Stucky handed her the keys. "Bring it back when you don't need it anymore." He laughed. "I know where to find you."

"I hope to be in Bakersfield for only a couple of days. I should be back on Thursday to help get ready for my father's wedding."

She was broke. Yet somehow, she'd find a way to do the thing that must be done.

After waving goodbye to her father and Louise, Jolene put Daddy's credit card into her wallet. He'd insisted she take it and buy whatever was needed for the reception. "Won't have you spending your money on us, little girl. Especially right now when you don't have a job."

She didn't tell him she might have to use it for additional expenses without his knowledge. She felt like a thief though he'd have gladly lent her the funds if he knew her plans. Too risky to divulge anything until she'd confronted Mary Ashworth.

Jolene prayed the entire thirty-minute drive to Bakersfield. The town had doubled in population since she left, most of the industries either owned by Ashworth Enterprises or backed by one or more of their financial institutions.

Fiddlers Fling

The county courthouse was a four-story red brick building, built in the early 1900s. The citizens of Bakersfield fought hard to keep the building in use, citing its significance as a historical landmark. The town's claim to fame—the murder trial of the notorious mobster Happy Delaney. The spectacle made national headlines for the entire six-month process, ending in a controversial conviction.

Jolene wished Nissie were back to work, uncertain if Cedric Landreau's temporary office manager could be trusted. Most county employees were honest people, but she feared the Ashworths had paid some of the staff as informants. *Lord, pave the way before me.*

Would Cedric be in his office? What if he'd gone out for lunch? Would he even agree to see her? If he didn't know about the breakup, he'd assume she was here for Ashworth business. All of Bakersfield knew Cedric Landreau's political preferences ran toward the opposite party, perhaps the reason he kept hitting brick walls on so many of his cases. The Ashworths would like nothing more than to see one of their paid lawyers sit in the DA's seat.

Jolene checked in at the first-floor security station. "My name is—"

"I know who you are."

"I have an appointment with Cedric Landreau."

"I'll let him know you're here."

Jolene held her breath while the woman called his office. "Mr. Landreau? I'm surprised you answered ... Oh, I forgot Lisa goes to lunch at this time. Anyway, this is Marnie at the front desk. Miss Murdock is here for her appointment. Shall I send her up?"

She listened a few seconds, then disconnected. "He'll see you now. District Attorney Landreau's office is a secure area. There's a buzzer outside the office door."

Perhaps she should have included Dwight in her plans, but in all likelihood, surveillance would never stop, whether she married Robert or not. Mary Ashworth would stoop to anything to keep Jolene under her thumb. If Mary discovered how much Jolene knew, no telling what the woman would do to those Jolene loved. She dared to breathe as she climbed the steps and offered a prayer of gratitude. Cedric waited for her and winked as if he expected her. Once in his office he shut the door, his face serene. "Don't look so surprised, Jolene. Nissie called me and said you'd be coming in today with information about the Fremont Women's

Clinic. I made sure none of my staff was around this morning, so we could talk freely." He looked at his cell. "I worried you might change your mind. Glad you didn't."

"I didn't tell anyone I was coming."

"Nissie said she was tipped by someone named Dwight Etting, a friend of her husband. Your friend too, I take it?"

Jolene nodded.

Cedric motioned for her to sit in the chair by his desk. He put his hands behind his head and leaned back in his swivel chair. Jolene quickly scanned the inner sanctum of Bakersfield's leading voice against political corruption. Credentials displayed against plain, off-white walls; piles of folders buried his massive, antique desk. Cedric, nearing retirement, had a full head of gray hair, neatly cropped. A thin, tallish African-American, his black eyes gleamed with sincerity. "I must admit, I was surprised when Nissie mentioned your estrangement from young Ashworth. I assume you're no longer working for their foundation."

"You assume correctly. Did Nissie explain why I hoped to see you?"

"Not specifically. Only that you had information that would help our case."

Jolene leaned back in her chair, took a deep breath, and slowly exhaled. "Seven years ago, I was a patient at the Fremont Clinic."

"That's interesting. I've been over the list of patients many times. I don't recall coming across your name."

"I was admitted under the alias, Denise Smith."

Cedric took out a file and thumbed through several pages of data. "Yes, here it is. There are a lot Smiths, Jones, and Johnsons listed. We assumed most of the patients used aliases. We've been investigating the clinic for ten years. The few patients we've been able to identify refuse to cooperate. You're the first person to come forward and admit you were there."

Jolene told Cedric the events of that night, how Mary Ashworth whisked her away from the pharmacy and brought her to the clinic, how she fawned over Jolene and insisted an abortion was the only reasonable solution. Jolene provided details of the procedure, as much as she remembered, how she was examined and told she was eight weeks pregnant and would require a harmless procedure that would only take a few minutes. A nurse inserted an IV, and Jolene was given general anesthesia. When she woke up, she was told it was all over. An aide brought her a glass of ginger ale. An hour later, she was told to get dressed and that Mrs. Ashworth would give her a ride home.

"I was a scared eighteen-year-old who foolishly believed Mary Ashworth was being kind. Funny thing, Cedric. In some ways, I came to love her like a mother, too naïve to realize she used my fear to manipulate me."

"And you're willing to testify? Why now?"

"Thing is ... I learned from Doc Benson that I was never pregnant. He's willing to give you an affidavit to that effect."

Cedric took out a recorder. "Let's start from the beginning once more."

Jolene leaned against the driver's seat, drained of all energy. Yet she also felt exonerated and filled with new purpose. She pulled out her newly purchased cell, courtesy of Michael Murdock's credit card, certain her father wouldn't have objected if he'd known she'd make this all-important contact. She was surprised Mary answered so quickly.

"Yes?"

"Hello, Mary. This is Jolene."

"My caller ID has this as Michael Murdock."

Jolene felt the heat as she spoke. "My father bought me a new phone since I can't use my old one anymore."

"Tell me you've called to let us know you've finally come to your senses."

"Yes, I have, but not the way you think. I thought you'd like to know that I've had an interesting conversation with Cedric Landreau."

Chapter Twenty-eight

Two weeks later

Thirty-six contestants crowded the registration tent at the county fairgrounds grandstand area. Jolene glanced at the seats, already nearly filled to capacity, the event a fairgrounds highlight since Jolene could remember. Her last competition had been the spring of her junior year of college, taking first place in the adult/child category with "Appalachia Waltz." Daddy had hoped they'd compete in the National Oldtime Fiddler's Contest the following year ... the year Jolene's life had changed forever.

He approached, a faint smile on his face. "Remember, little girl, don't let the fiddle slide." He pulled her aside. "I'm grateful to the Almighty I'll have this memory to share with your mother when I see her."

Louise sidled next to Daddy. "I heard that, Michael."

Daddy pecked her on the cheek. "Don't worry none, Mrs. Murdock. You and Babs will be great friends."

Louise laughed. "We'll make an interesting quartet up there with our late spouses, won't we?"

Jolene smiled to herself as she remembered Daddy and Louise's wedding. Only a week ago, yet they seemed as if they'd been married for years. The ceremony had been a small affair, with Dwight and Jolene serving as witnesses and a few guests dropping by the house afterward. Still, Daddy hadn't wasted the opportunity for a jam session, insisting those who could play an instrument should bring it with them. The place filled with memories of former days when music from the Murdock house spilled into the streets of Brookside.

The group event was first. Murdock Madness, as they called themselves, took the stage to a hearty applause. Her father had chosen "David's Jig," one of Jolene's favorites. Toes tapped, and several couples standing outside the stands danced a reel.

She'd fumbled in a few places, her lack of practice over the last three years evident. Yet surprisingly she'd kept up better than she'd hoped. Not good enough for a first-place finish, but perhaps they'd place in the top five.

The next sets were junior players and adult/junior duets. The sight of the children playing with their parents brought Jolene back in time. She'd been blessed with a father who loved her unconditionally. Though he rarely spoke his affection, he lavished it on her, his scolding and occasional punishment laced with love. She'd been the stubborn one, rebellion her middle name. She lifted a prayer of thanks that God brought her back home in time to know her father's love once again.

Dwight tapped her on the shoulder. "You're up for the duet, Jolene."

As they took their places for "The Devil Went Down to Georgia," Daddy motioned to watch for the changes and to follow his lead. They finished to a standing ovation and wild applause. Flawless. An approving smile spread across her father's face, accentuating his sunken cheeks.

As they exited the stage, he pulled her aside. "You make me proud, little girl. I want you to know that. Promise me you'll never put your fiddle down again. It's a sin to waste the talent God gave you." He ambled to where Louise waited and kissed her hand.

Jolene put her fiddle away. She was surprised that Daddy, usually the first to pack up, still held onto his.

Dwight joined her. "Big Mike made a last-minute entry into the solo category."

She raised her eyebrows in surprise as the emcee came to the platform. "Our first contestant in this last round is no stranger to this competition, a twenty-time champion, and county favorite. Let's hear it for Big Mike Murdock, who'll be playing the 'Ashokan Farewell.'"

Tears streamed down several faces as he played, the significance more than Jolene could bear. The melody, written to commemorate the Civil War, symbolized the eternal struggle within each soul. When he rested his bow at the highest treble note, a holy hush descended upon the stands, as if angels gathered to hear a preview of what heaven would gain. No one dared to clap lest the celestial visitation be disturbed.

Daddy bowed and walked off the stage, his staggering exit a sign he'd never raise his fiddle again until he played it for the Lord.

Sometimes a man had to weep. Big Mike must have played that song a hundred times but never as beautifully as today. Dwight took Jolene's hand in his. "That was for you, Jolene. Big Mike wants you to know he's okay."

She wiped her tears. "I sensed that."

"I have to go back to my apartment and take care of Sandy. Afterward, I thought I'd ride over on the ATV. Maybe we can take your new and improved Raptor out for a spin." He suspected he might need to use more persuasion, surprised when she gave no argument. He smiled as he continued. "I'm leaving now. Let me know where we placed when I get to your house."

She nodded. "The day I came back to Brookside, I didn't feel like it was my home anymore."

"And now?"

"According to my father it is, has been, and always will be my house. He added my name to the deed when I turned twenty-one."

He tugged his cap and walked to his truck, Big Mike's performance still vibrating in his heart—comforted with a presence, one he'd tried to ignore for the past few weeks. "No more war, Lord." He'd already forgiven Jolene, his love for her greater than the rift that threatened to keep them apart.

He fed Sandy, took her out for a brief walk, changed into comfortable riding clothes and then pocketed his mother's ring. As he started toward the door, Sandy barked. He turned, and she ran into his arms. He rubbed her sides and neck. "Wish me luck, girl."

Still wearing the fitted rhinestone-studded jeans Big Mike bought her for the contest, Jolene stepped from the house as Dwight pulled into the drive. Desire filled him, deeper than any he'd known. He wanted to greet each new day with her by his side, to create harmonies to last a lifetime. They belonged together. Always did. He hoped she'd see that now.

She put on her helmet and coasted her Raptor out of the garage. "Stucky's my hero. A miracle-worker for sure."

"Sometimes things aren't as lost as they seem."

"Guess not."

"Before we start, how did we do?"

"Murdock Madness took third place, our duet, second, and Daddy, of course, took first."

"No surprise there."

Jolene tightened her helmet strap. "Where are we riding to?"

"Let's take the path to the river and watch the sunset."

"Okay."

They rode over narrow trails to their once favorite landing. The sun began its descent and scattered speckles of orange across a clear sky. They dismounted and sat on the rock ledge.

Dwight held her hand. "I've been a fool, Jolene."

"Join the club."

"I had no right to judge you."

"You couldn't have been as hard on me as I was on myself."

"I know I told you not to go to Bakersfield without me. But I'm proud of you. It took a lot of guts to do what you did."

"I read in the paper this morning that Robert has withdrawn from the senatorial race."

Dwight laughed. "They'll find a way to spin this whole thing in due time."

She nodded in agreement. "Cedric Landreau told me the Ashworths agreed to a plea bargain. They'll have to pay millions in fines as well as commit to several years of community service. No jail time, though. But the clinic stays closed for good."

"That explains their large contribution to the nursing home project."

"That was in exchange for a media gag order. Their crimes will never make headlines, but at least they won't prey on girls in trouble ever again. They gave the clinic property to a Christian crisis pregnancy support group."

Perhaps all things do work together for good. He turned his gaze across the river. "See those pike jumping?"

She peered toward the horizon. "Yes. I've always loved this spot at sunset."

"I may not have a lot of time for riding in the upcoming weeks."

"Business booming? That's great."

"It's a lot of work."

"No kidding."

"I could use some help."

"You're CEO—hire as much help as you need."

He cleared his throat. "Here's an idea. Why don't you put your old tool belt on and come join the fun?"

"I'd like to."

"What's stopping you?"

Her eyes mirrored uncertainty. "I'm not sure our working together every day is a good idea. We're just becoming friends again. I don't want to mess that up."

He reached out and pulled her close, and their lips met, though he felt awkward, like when he kissed her for the first time. He rose, then helped her up from the rock ledge to a face-to-face standing position. With his eyes locked on hers, he fell to one knee. "I'm not good at speeches, Jolene." He took out the ring from his pocket. "This was my mother's. Before she died, she told me I should give it to you when the time was right. Guess somehow she knew I'd always love you."

Tears shone in Jolene's eyes as she answered in an awestruck whisper. "I've always loved you too."

Dwight tried to stifle his grin, but it was impossible. "If that's the case," he said, "don't you think it's time we got married?"

Epilogue

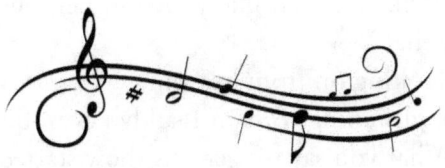

Jolene stood in front of the mirror, tilting her head to one side as she examined the full impact of the tea-length, a white laced dress designed and sewn by Louise Murdock. She'd crafted a matching headpiece and trimmed it with white roses. *She should add seamstress to her growing list of talents. The woman is far too modest.*

She smiled as she thought how this wedding would be the antithesis of the one she thought she'd have when she left Albany. Same day, different venue, different groom, yet a celebration she much preferred over an Ashworth circus.

The day had become a complete flip-flop. According to the paper, Robert was marrying Alicia Davenport today. Interesting that even an Ashworth didn't want to waste good money. Same plans, different bride ... What did it matter to them as long as it remained the party of the decade?

Nissie Mahoney, Jolene's matron of honor, stepped inside Pastor Tim's study, stunning in her lavender tea-length, set off by a miniature bouquet of pink roses. "Need help?"

"I think I'm set."

"You're glowing, Jolene. I felt the same way when I married Jack. Completely at peace that he was the one for me."

Peace ... finally. God was so good. "How's Dwight holding up?"

"Jack said he'd never seen a man more ready to get married."

Jolene smiled. "We've been ready since the third grade when we held a mock wedding in my backyard."

Fiddlers Fling

The muted knock, weak yet firm, could only be Daddy's. "Come in," Jolene called.

His once white Santa Claus hair, now yellowed by disease, shone against the vibrant gray suit he'd worn for his own recent wedding.

"Daddy, you are one handsome dude."

He smiled, his eyes bright with pride. "Glad I have an occasion to wear this at least one more time before my funeral. Cost me enough."

"Daddy! No sad thoughts today. Promise?"

"Promise. You look so much like your mother. She wore her hair up and curled just like that."

"I'm sure she's looking on from heaven."

She spotted the glistening tears in Daddy's eyes, but he blinked them away and asked, "What you say we get this show started?"

"Sure you're up to this?"

"I'll crawl to the altar if I have to. My privilege to give you away … especially to Dwight."

She took her father's arm, finding strength from his love though his legs could barely carry him. Jolene scanned the church. Among the two dozen guests were District Attorney Cedric Landreau and Mayor Billings, both inviting themselves, perhaps in rebellion against the Ashworths.

The worship team sang "Love Will Be Our Home" for the processional while individual pictures of the bride and groom—from childhood, college, the Army, and the recent Fiddlers Fling—flashed on the overhead screen. The wedding plans were so rushed there had been no time to decorate. Jolene marveled at the tufts of lavender chiffon adorning the pews and the two floral baskets at the altar, donated by the Ladies Prayer Circle. How could she ever have wanted to leave Brookside?

Her father presented her to Dwight, then took a seat next to Louise as Pastor Tim began.

"Dearly Beloved … "

After the opening remarks, Jolene followed Dwight's lead onto the platform. Could she get through this duet without cracking with emotion, harmonizing to "Bless the Broken Road?" Their individual paths seemed destined to lead them apart, yet through twists and turns neither could have imagined, God brought them back to an all-important intersection.

When they retook their place at the altar, Pastor Tim continued. "The bride and groom have written their own vows. Jolene?"

"Dwight Etting, you have always been my rock. I asked God to send me a husband like Big Mike Murdock. The Lord not only heard that prayer but has answered it in you. I'm grateful for a father who has never stopped loving me, even when I rebelled ... for a town that embodies all that is good about America ... and for you, Dwight, my best friend in life. Most of all I'm grateful to the Lord, who has orchestrated our union today. I promise from this day forward, with the Lord's help, to be your companion, to love, honor, and obey, for richer, for poorer, in sickness and in health, until death parts us." She placed the ring on Dwight's finger.

Pastor Tim turned to face Dwight. "Dwight Etting, do you take this woman to be your wife?"

With only a slight trembling in his voice, he began. "I do. Jolene, I never could put two sentences together without stuttering, except when I'm with you. We speak a language unique to us. I've loved you since we were babies. You're the source of my joy, the melody in my song. From this day forward, with the Lord's help, I promise to cherish only you, for richer, for poorer, in sickness and in health, until death parts us."

Jack Mahoney came to the platform and sang "This Ring," then Pastor Tim raised his hands to the congregation. "By the power vested in me by this church and the State of New York, I now pronounce you husband and wife. Let no one put asunder what God has brought together."

They held hands and step-danced down the aisle to Jack and the worship band's "David's Jig." The congregation joined in the dance as they made their way to congratulate the bride and groom.

Dwight leaned in and kissed her. "Hello, Mrs. Etting."

She returned his kiss. "This might be as good a time as any to tell you my surprise."

Dwight raised his brows. "I knew this marriage would never have a dull moment. What surprise?"

"We—Daddy and I—changed the company name to Etting & Etting."

He kissed her. "I like the sound of that. It echoes."

THE END

Discussion Questions for Christian Women's Groups/Book Clubs

Why do you think Jolene felt compelled to go through with her marriage to Robert, even though she had doubts?

How would you counsel a young woman whose boyfriend or fiancé demands her to change to suit him or his family?

How can the church prevent abortions? What can the church do to help someone heal who has had an abortion?

Jolene and her father were estranged for several years. What keeps families broken? How can the church help?

Jolene and Dwight grew up in the church. Do you think there is a risk for church kids to grow up thinking they are Christians because their parents are? How can the church help young people realize their own accountability for their faith?

Ultimately, it is music that brings Jolene back to her roots, to herself, and to true salvation. How important do you think music is in your church? How can the music ministry be improved? How does your church manage cross-generational music preferences?

Fiddlers Fling

Big Mike's problems became lost when the church underwent pastoral change. Should the church continue ministering to absentees? How can this be effectively managed, especially when a church is in transition?

Dwight found His faith after being wounded in Afghanistan. Share with the group: What non-church experiences have brought you closer to the Lord?

Big Mike is terminally ill. What does your church do to minister to the sick? Are current programs meeting needs? If not, what could be different?

Jolene turned for guidance outside the church when she found herself in trouble. Why do you think young people fail to seek counseling from the church for life's problems? What do you think the church can do to support youth in crisis.

About the Author

LINDA WOOD RONDEAU

God is able to turn our worst past into our best future. This is the theme of every Rondeau book. A veteran social worker, Rondeau delves into the intricacies of human relationships, earning her critical acclaim for her heart-warming stories of deliverance and forgiveness. The author now resides in Hagerstown, MD with her best friend in life, her husband of forty years. Active in her local church, she enjoys playing the occasional round of golf, a common feature in many of her books. Readers may contact the author through Facebook, Twitter, Goodreads, Google Plus, Pinterest, and Instagram or visit her website: www.lindarondeau.com.

www.ingramcontent.com/pod-product-compliance
Lightning Source LLC
Chambersburg PA
CBHW072102170626
46813CB00004B/1433